FAKE

PUSHKIN CHILDREN'S

Pushkin Press
71–75 Shelton Street
London WC2H 9JQ

Fake was first published by Pushkin Press in 2022

1 3 5 7 9 8 6 4 2

ISBN 13: 978-1-78269-290-4

Designed and typeset by Tetragon, London
Printed and bound by CPI Group (UK) Ltd, Croydon, CRO 4YY

www.pushkinpress.com

Contents

For Isabelle, Oliver and Sophia

You cannot buy the revolution.
You cannot make the revolution.
You can only be the revolution.
It is in your spirit, or it is nowhere.

URSULA K. LE GUIN
The Dispossessed

End

'Shirts?'

'Yes.'

'Socks?'

'Yes.'

'Pants!'

I look up and see Chloe grinning next to Mum.

'Well, you'll need pants,' she adds.

I try to glare but end up smiling.

It's hard to glare at Chloe. Also, this time tomorrow I will be gone. I turn back to the wooden trunk, my possessions piled within, including pants.

No one else will have a trunk like mine. There is an entire section of ROOM devoted to school kit. Especially luggage. Luggage which weighs itself, keeps itself cool, keeps warm, transports itself. I am almost relieved that I have no choice in the matter.

Mine opens and closes. That's it. I lower the heavy lid. It doesn't quite match up with the rest of the trunk, so I put my foot on top and press down. It still doesn't close. I guess it just opens then.

'That's an heirloom,' Chloe reminds me.

'I thought you had to be dead before your things became heirlooms. Dad is in the kitchen making pancakes.'

On cue, a disembodied voice calls, 'Does someone need me?'

I sigh. 'I just wish this trunk wasn't so—big. Or grey.'

'We could paint it!' Chloe cries. 'Purple! With yellow stars.'

Mum is watching me. She puts down the list. 'Come on, Chloe, let's go out and pick some lettuce for lunch.'

Chloe hops up and grabs Mum's outstretched hand. 'Rainbow stripes?' she shouts from the kitchen.

I take the list from the arm of the chair where Mum left it. We've been through it a thousand times. Once was enough. I know there's nothing missing. Even so, I scan through one last time, then sit in the chair and stare at the trunk. I should be making the most of every last second with my family. For some reason I want to be on my own.

I've looked forward to this day for fourteen years. Now that it's here, the butterflies in my stomach have gone, leaving behind a strange, empty feeling. Instead of wondering who I'll make friends with first, I find myself thinking about Chloe. About whispering goodnight from the top bunk. About crating up the apples and harvesting the honeycomb. About herding the goats to their pen in the low evening sun. Mum brushing my hair from my eyes. Dad brushing his hair from his eyes when we play chess. About Finn.

It's annoying.

Shock

'Jess?'

The voice startles me. I drop my toothbrush in the sink. In the mirror a pale face with grey smudges beneath the eyes, hovers behind my right shoulder. Most of the time, you would never guess Chloe was ill. Sometimes, like now, the reality seems closer to the surface.

'Sorry, I thought you heard me get up.'

I shake my head and pick up my toothbrush.

'Will we have time to go down to the treehouse before you leave?'

We don't have time, but I nod my head anyway. I finish brushing then grab my portal watch and try connecting to Finn. Seconds later a sleepy face topped with messy brown hair appears on the small screen. Chloe leans in to look.

'I am so glad you called,' he says sleepily. 'Mum's working and I didn't hear my alarm. I could have missed my first day completely.'

'Treehouse in ten?'

Finn rubs his left eye with his free hand. 'What? I haven't even finished packing.'

'If it wasn't for me you'd still be asleep. Come on. I'll bring breakfast.'

Before he can argue I disconnect.

Chloe squeals with excitement.

'Grab your hoodie,' I say, 'it's cold outside.'

We creep downstairs. Soft morning light blooms around the edge of the kitchen door. As I push it open, warm cooking aromas waft out.

'I was just coming to check you were ready.' Dad looks up from the hob. 'Scrambled egg?'

Dad is always up early, just normally outside with the animals. He'll say there's no time for the treehouse.

'Chlo and I were going to let the goats out.'

'Scrambled egg in a bun?'

'Yeah!' says Chloe.

'Can I have two? I'm really hungry.'

Dad slices three buns and stuffs them to bursting, before wrapping a piece of beeswax paper round the outside.

I pull on a pair of wellies and Chloe lifts the latch on the door.

The morning air smells like cut grass. Pale blue sky is tinged with a sunrise glow where it meets the hills.

The cockerel calls nearby as Chloe marches ahead past neat rows of winter vegetable seedlings, and the rich brown soil from which we harvested peas, beans and carrots. Beyond is a meadow, with a miniature village of beehives.

I take a bite from the soft roll with its warm filling. As we cross the meadow, there is another scent in the air—of damp leaves. Of summer turning to autumn.

The field dips to meet a line of oak trees. As we approach, I spot a figure running down the hill opposite, arms spread like the sails of a wind turbine.

At the base of the largest oak dangles a rope. Chloe gives a tug, and a ladder tumbles down, parallel to the trunk. She climbs up, disappearing beyond the leaves of a low branch. I wait at the bottom, clutching a scrambled-egg roll.

Footsteps thud across the nearby ground. Moments later a boy lurches into the clearing.

He sees me and grins, then bends forwards, hands on knees, trying to catch his breath. After a few seconds, he pants, 'Breakfast?'

I pass him the roll, now only a few centimetres thick, with a large dip where my thumb pressed down.

He wolfs it in a couple of bites.

'Thanks. Any more?' He looks hopefully at my hands.

'Sorry, the chef doesn't take bulk orders.'

'Are you coming?' A voice floats down from the canopy.

I steady the rope ladder with my right hand and begin to climb. Once I'm above the lowest branches, the ladder sways as Finn follows.

The top rung marks the entrance to a small wooden shelter, nestled in the 'v' where the massive trunk diverges. Each plank has been shaped so perfectly, it looks as if the tree was bored one day and instead of branches, grew a hut.

I climb inside and wait as my eyes adjust to the gloom. Light filters through two canopied windows.

There are bean bags, a low bench, and at the back a few wooden boxes with snacks and any other stuff we might need. Finn squeezes in behind me.

'Hey, Chlo!'

She grins at him, eyes shining in the dim light.

'What's that?' she asks.

Finn is clutching a small bundle which I hadn't noticed until now. He passes it to her.

'For you.'

She takes the bundle with two hands.

'Should I open it?'

'Definitely not.'

'Then what should I do with it?' she frowns.

'Open it after we've gone. I don't want you moping around, so I've made a few things to keep you busy.'

A smile creeps slowly towards the dimples in her cheeks.

'There's a treasure hunt, and some puzzles. There's also a secret code. Only you, me and Jess will have the cypher.'

'The what?'

'The cypher—the way to work out what it means. That way we can send messages to each other and no one will be able to read them. By no one, I mean your mum and dad.'

As Chloe turns the package over in her hands, hot tears well in the corners of my eyes. I blink them away.

'She'll be too busy to miss us,' I add. 'Mum and Dad are going to need extra help for my jobs, and then she'll have to look after Kit, too.'

'Kit?' asks Finn.

Chloe and I exchange a look.

'It's all right, Chlo, I think you can tell him. He won't share.'

'Kit's a kitten. Mum and Dad found her near the composter. I waited nearby for the mother to return. After two days, there was no sign, and Kit was starving. We couldn't just let her die.'

Finn sucks air in over his teeth. 'Keeping a pet. That's an offence, Miss Chloe. I hope you like prison food.'

Chloe giggles.

'Mum says when she was little everyone had pets.'

'I guess one more animal round your house isn't exactly going to stand out,' adds Finn, grinning, 'even if pets *are* illegal.'

He glances at his port-watch, then leaps up, banging his head on the roof.

'I really *really* have to pack, or else I'll be turning up in the clothes I'm wearing and nothing else,' he says, rubbing the top of his head.

'Look after everyone, Chloe.' He bends to give her a hug. 'Bye, Jess.' He puts his arms around me and squeezes. His messy brown hair is the last thing I see as he climbs down the ladder. 'Send me messages!' he calls up.

'I will!' Chloe stares at the hole through which Finn disappeared moments before. She lifts the lid from the largest wooden box and places the package gently inside, then turns towards the rope ladder and follows Finn down.

My port-watch vibrates. The word MUM flashes on the screen.

'We're coming!' I say to my wrist, before Mum can speak.

I clamber down as fast as I can in oversized wellies, then tug the rope, raising the ladder above the canopy, out of sight.

When I turn round, Chloe is already ten metres away, running through the field.

'Chloe, slow down!' I shout. I feel a thrill of fear in my stomach.

Morning sun slices through the trees, scattering sparkles across the dewy grass. I stomp after her, running as fast as my wellies allow.

'Let me catch you up!' I call, trying to think of a way to make her stop.

Finn's parcel or the sunshine or both seem to have filled her with a new kind of energy.

She reaches the brow of the hill, and begins to slow. I run alongside and reach for her hand.

'Walk with me for a bit?' I pant. 'I accidentally put Mum's wellies on and they're way too big for running.'

We walk side by side. My breathing gradually slows, but Chloe's does not. I glance over. Her face is white, her lips pale. We are only halfway to the house. I try not to panic.

'How about a piggyback? You won't have the chance again for a while.'

She doesn't answer. Her breath is catching in her throat with a wheezy rattle.

I bend down and she clambers onto my back. She feels much lighter than she looks. Her arms drape over my shoulders and I feel her head resting near the back of my neck. I start to jog, not caring about the wellies.

As I reach the edge of the meadow, my muscles are beginning to burn. I pin Chloe's legs against me so that she doesn't slip. I pass the beehives, and when the house comes into view, there is a figure by the back door.

'Mum!' I try to shout, but it comes out like a loud gasp. 'Mum!' I try again. She lifts her head and walks slowly towards me. When she spots Chloe on my back, she stops in her tracks, then runs back to the house. She leans through the door, shouting something to Dad.

I stagger in behind her, feeling Dad lift Chloe from my shoulders. He takes her to the sofa and props her upright on the cushions. She cannot speak; her eyes are wide with fear. She watches Dad as he pulls something from a box by the sofa. Her breathing is fast and shallow, and there is a soft wheezing sound every time her chest moves up and down. Her lips are bluish. Dad places a see-through plastic mask over Chloe's nose and mouth and presses a pump at the side. The mask fills with cloudy vapour.

Mum sits down next to Chloe. We wait.

Dad looks at his port-watch. After a minute or so, Chloe's breathing hasn't slowed. There is a low hiss as he presses the pump again.

I kneel on the floor next to Chloe and take her hand. I draw shapes on the back of it, like I do when she can't get to sleep.

Chloe's shoulders move up and down more slowly. Her face is pale, but the fear has left her eyes.

'What happened?' Dad asks gently, as we sit.

'We went down to the treehouse.' I hesitate. 'I knew there wasn't time. We met Finn there. He had some things for Chloe. We ran back up the hill. It's my fault.'

Dad puts his arm round me. 'Chloe's going to be OK. That's more important than whose fault it was.' I feel tears rising again and blink them away. I don't want to upset Chloe. 'We'll just have to take it easy for a few days.' Dad looks at Chloe. Her eyes are closed now.

'Jess,' Mum says quietly, 'I'm sorry, but we need to go. The transport is charged. Dad's put your trunk in the trailer.

'Chloe and I will have to stay here,' says Dad, even though it's obvious they can't go anywhere.

I nod. I know how much Chloe was looking forward to coming. How much I wanted her to see my home for the next five years.

I lean over to give her a kiss on the forehead. She stirs and opens her eyes.

'Make sure Mum and Dad behave,' I whisper. 'Let me know if they cause any trouble.'

She nods.

I feel like a magnet pulled in two directions. Hovering in between makes my head spin. I have to go; I need to go, but I don't want to leave Chloe. Especially not now.

As I reach the doorway, Dad says softly, 'Remember, Jess. The other children will have led very different lives to you. Be careful what you share with them. Until you know them a little better.'

I nod, not quite trusting my voice to work properly. He wraps his arms around me and I breathe in the baking bread smell from his jumper. Tomorrow everything will still be here. Our house will be the same, only I won't be in it.

Beginning

'I can see it!'

I lean over to peer through Mum's window.

'No, other side,' she adds.

A large wooden structure emerges through the trees to our left, solar panels glinting on the roof.

The knot of excitement in my stomach twists a little tighter.

We turn down a narrow road, the building growing larger, its true size obscured by trees and bushes planted either side. As we approach, I see a row of transports parked opposite. All with trailers attached. No transport has space for luggage—big transports waste electricity. But for special trips, there are trailers. Families used to have massive cars which could carry everything. Transports only have room for seats, to save energy.

People are piling luggage on the ground, hugging each other goodbye. There must be at least ten groups, maybe more. By the entrance, a similar number of children filter slowly through the enormous doors. I've never seen so many people in my life. Not real people.

'Right, let's get your trunk out!'

I realize that our transport has stopped.

'Do you have your violin?'

Mum's voice is too bright. Too happy for unloading a trunk or locating a violin. But I'm glad, because I suddenly feel shaky, and her bright voice makes it seem as if everything will be OK.

We heave the trunk on to the gravel, from where someone is supposed to collect it. Mum hugs me.

'Be bold. Question everything. Don't forget to brush your teeth.'

'I won't have any trouble with the middle one,' I say.

'You won't have any trouble at all,' says Mum.

She turns back to the transport. Parents aren't supposed to come as far as the entrance. Mum gives a little wave, even though she's only a few metres away, then climbs inside.

I crunch slowly across the gravel towards the enormous doors. The sun feels warm on the back of my head, casting an orange glow on the huge wood-panelled walls.

Halfway, I turn to watch our silver transport glide along the winding road. Every second, a little smaller. Until I am the furthest I have ever been from my family in my entire life. It will be one whole week before I'm even allowed to speak to them again.

At the door, there are still three children making their way in. I can't believe we will be sharing rooms. Sharing lessons. Sitting next to each other.

After fourteen years of waiting, I am at school.

Real

'Move to the front! There's plenty of space.'

Instinctively, I search for a screen, but the voice belongs to an actual person. A woman standing on a small stage at the far end of the hall. She is smiling warmly and waving her arms to beckon people in. I seem to be among the last to arrive. At least fifty students are already seated. I hurry forwards, then sidle along one of the rows towards a girl with short black hair. She looks at me, eyes wide with fright. I leave several seats between us. Mum warned me that some students will never have met another child before. Despite all the preparation exercises, they might be nervous.

Apart from the sound of footsteps and people shifting in their seats, the room is quiet.

'Welcome, everyone, I am your principal,' says the

woman. She's wearing a dark blue jumper, the same shade as our chicken house. Chloe would like that.

'I know you've been waiting a long time for this day. Many of you will feel excited, many of you will feel nervous, too. However strange things might seem now, I promise that in a few weeks, this will feel like home.'

No one murmurs.

The lady explains that first, we will go to our dormitories. There are three for the boys and three for the girls. Our luggage will be next to our beds. Then, once we've met our roommates, there will be lunch followed by a tour of the school.

'When your name is called, please exit via the door through which you entered.'

Another woman appears, clutching a small device from which she reads out names. One by one, students get to their feet and walk down the central aisle. They snatch glances. No one makes eye contact.

Their clothes look brand new; exciting. Some change colour to match the surroundings, others have muscle-activator pads, which keep you fit while you're sitting still. I'm wearing my favourite jumper and trousers. They have changed colour, but only because they've been washed so much. The girl with short dark hair stands up. She has the same wide-eyed expression as when I arrived. I think she might be working out how to leave without walking past me. I turn sideways, allowing as much space as possible for her to pass.

I'm wondering whether I will be last, when finally my name is called. I sidle along the chairs, arriving in the central aisle at the same time as a girl with wavy auburn hair. Instead of looking away, she stares right at me. Her hazel-green eyes flit around my face. I realize that I am staring at her in the same way, and we both smile.

'Follow the purple arrows,' calls the lady with the list. She walks briskly towards us, along with the final few students.

The corridor glows with light from solar magnifiers overhead. Footsteps tap along the smooth floor. We follow purple arrows right then left, across a courtyard, and into what looks like an enormous sitting room, although the sign on the door says *Common Room*.

I keep walking, up a wide flight of stairs, towards another door labelled *Dormitory*. The facial recognition scanner blinks and it slides open to reveal a huge L-shaped room, stretching away towards a large window. Ten beds line the walls, wardrobes and comfy-looking chairs scattered between.

Several girls hover near the door, as if the room might bite. I see my trunk over by the window. It's easy to spot. Beside every other bed are sleek-looking bags and brand-new cases.

As I head towards my things, the other girls disperse in search of their beds, too.

'Where's the screen?' someone asks in a shaky voice. It belongs to the girl with black hair, the one I'd sat next to in the hall.

It's true, there doesn't seem to be a screen of any kind, but then I wasn't expecting one. After eight years of virtual live-learning, I thought school was where we came to have real lessons with real teachers. Dad's words echo in my head. *The other children will have led very different lives to you.*

'I wish they could give us a virtual tour instead of a real tour,' she adds, perching on a chair near the middle of the room. Her voice is no longer shaky. She sounds slightly annoyed.

There is a sniff from the bed next to me. A girl with curly blonde hair wipes a tear from her cheek and stares at her shiny turquoise case; the name Ana sparkles in silvery letters near the handle. I think about what I might say to Chloe, if she was feeling sad. I'm about to open my mouth when Ana holds up her port-watch and scans the case, then lifts her wrist higher, moving it left to right as she takes a panoramic of the dormitory. I know she will be adding it to ROOM, the 3D virtual reality space where you can show off what's in your wardrobe, or new make-up, or anything you want to share. It has to be new though, so that you can link it to the store where you bought it. Curating your ROOM includes decorating or choosing themes too. You can spend hours on it. Everyone uses ROOM and collects ROOMmates. Well, almost everyone.

A voice from across the dormitory breaks the awkward silence which has fallen.

'It looks like we're going to be sleeping next to each other. I hope you don't snore. I'm Mae, by the way.'

It's the girl with auburn hair. Her neighbour lowers her port-watch. She was also scanning her luggage. Now she shrinks back, as if Mae might be dangerous.

Everyone in the room has stopped what they are doing to watch.

'I was only joking about the snoring,' says Mae, who must have noticed the girl's reaction. 'What's your name?'

'It's Eve,' she whispers, looking studiously at her bedspread. She's at least a head taller than Mae, but seems to have retreated into a more compact version of herself.

Mae appears encouraged by the response. 'I'm so hungry,' she adds. 'Is anyone else ready for lunch?' This comment seems to be directed to the whole room.

'Yes!' I hear myself say. Nine pairs of eyes swivel my way.

Eve whispers something I can't hear.

'Sorry, what's that?' says Mae.

I can't help leaning forwards to catch the reply.

'Do you think we should take our healthplan supplements to lunch?' she repeats, even more quietly.

'Errr,' says Mae, looking over at me, for some reason.

But I don't need to say anything, because at that moment the door slides open and list-lady enters.

'I'm sure you're all very hungry after such a long morning,' she says, beaming. 'Follow me to the dining hall. Today you will eat with the other S1 dormitories. From tomorrow, you will eat with the rest of the school.'

I feel relieved it's just us. I'm not ready to meet the entire school. Not yet.

Secret

'How much more?' Mae yawns. 'I'm not sure I can walk down another corridor or take in any further Safety Aspects.'

We are sitting in the common room with Eve. The other girls have gone up to the dormitory. We've seen every room, heard every regulation, been through every cyber-rule. At least that's how it feels. But there hasn't been much chance to talk. I wonder if the school arranges it that way on purpose. Less pressure on the first day.

I hadn't realized how much Chloe and I chat when we're at home. Even though I feel more tired than I've ever felt in my life, I'm not ready for sleep.

'I think there's "Getting ready for bed", then "FOG",' I say reading the list on my port-watch.

'Getting ready for bed sounds straightforward,' says Mae. 'But what's FOG?'

'Hang on.'

A cloud of water droplets suspended in the atmosphere, my port-watch replies in a soothing tone.

'Here it means feet-off-the-ground,' a voice says quietly.

I glance at Eve in surprise. She immediately looks back down at her hands.

'Thank you, Eve,' I say. 'But what does feet-off-the-ground mean?'

A small smile flickers across her face. 'I think it means you have to be in bed.'

'Ohhh,' Mae and I say at the same time.

'What do you think so far?' Mae asks.

Eve's smile fades.

'It seems all right,' Mae adds.

Eve nods, hugging her long legs more closely to her chest. I'm not sure she wants to be the centre of attention.

'Do you have any brothers or sisters?' Mae persists.

'A younger brother,' says Eve, glancing up at Mae.

'Did you meet any other kids before you came here?'

Eve frowns. 'You mean, on live-learning?'

Mae hesitates. 'Yes, on live-learning.'

'No one from my live-learning class has come here. I don't recognize anyone. They all went to a different school.'

'No one from my live-learning is here either,' I say. I know that most of Finn's group has gone to his school. At least there will be kids he recognizes. Kids he's been live-learning with for the last eight years. Even if he's never actually met them. I wonder whether he's doing the same stuff we are today. Safety Aspects.

'I don't have any brothers or sisters.'

I look around the room to see where the voice is coming from. Sitting on a chair near the window, her knees tucked up to her chin, is the black-haired girl.

'I've never sat in a room with other kids. Real ones. Until today. My dad's a big tech director though, so we have the best hologram system available.'

'How about you, Mae?' I ask.

'How about me what?'

'Brothers and sisters? People you know here?'

'I have a sister. No live-learning friends. I didn't really do live-learning.'

'What?' the black-haired girl and I say together.

'It's no big deal,' says Mae. I notice that she is now the one who won't meet people's eyes. She must know that we are all looking at her though because she adds, 'I mean, well, I took the live-learning exams.' She draws a shape on the chair with her fingertip. 'I passed with top marks. I just didn't do the lessons.' She looks up.

'Shall we get ready for bed? I'm so tired I could sleep until next weekend.'

But she'll have to make do with one night. Because tomorrow is Monday. Our first day of lessons with an actual class in an actual school. With actual people.

I know it hasn't always been this way. People used to mix freely. You could play with friends who lived nearby. You could go to school when you were four. Mum and Dad talk to me and Chloe about what it was like when they were little. We've read books, and watched old films, too. They describe life before the Scarlet Fever outbreak which was the start of complete antibiotic resistance. Before cuts and grazes and stomach bugs became something to fear. Before any serious infection could kill you, and we had to stay at home until we were fourteen and our immune systems were strong enough to cope with almost anything.

Chloe and I shouldn't hang out with Finn. We met without our parents realizing, and by the time they did, it seemed pointless to stop us. That is our family secret.

But I have a secret too.

Secret 2

The main light dims, and a pale glow appears along the wall above each bed. I perch on the edge of the soft mattress, brushing my hair. I glance over to Ana's bed. In the middle of her pillow is a tangle of blonde hair. I can't see her face, but her shoulders rise and fall softly beneath the duvet. The housemaster will be here in a minute to enforce FOG, but she will have nothing to do. Everyone is busy sleeping, exhausted from a day of real people.

I slip my feet beneath the covers and lie down. The housemaster must not guess that I am busy staying awake.

I stare at the shadowy ceiling. There are no silver stars, painted by me and Chloe as we balanced on Dad's stepladder. Under my breath, I whisper, 'Goodnight, Chloe.' A little part of me wonders if, somehow, she will hear. Mum or Dad will sleep on the floor next to her tonight, like they always do when she's had a bad day. To check on her breathing. They must be careful to get her medication just right. Not enough, and she might have another episode in the night. But they can't afford to waste any. It's the most expensive thing our family buys. Running out would be unthinkable. We can't afford hospital.

Dad gave up commercial farming so that he could spend time with me and Chloe, instead of working in someone else's fields. We always have enough to eat, but there is never much spare. My parents save credits to buy medicine, and if there's anything left–shoes.

I look at my port-watch. Thirty minutes have passed. The housemaster has been and gone, and I didn't even notice.

I listen. The only sound is calm, steady breathing, the rhythms overlapping. No one stirs. I wait a few more minutes.

I am so tired, but I can't go to sleep. Not yet.

I think about the code which Finn gave to me and Chloe. Our secret code. We've been friends for ever, but there is one thing I have never shared with him, or Chloe. It must be a secret here, too.

As quietly as I can, I push my covers away and step on the soft floor tiles. Ana stirs. After a few seconds,

I move again, crouching next to my bed. Gently, I open the drawer beneath my mattress. It slides towards me on smooth, silent runners. I reach inside and take out a thin, rectangular object. My port-com. No one has a port-com like this any more. I don't even know if you can buy them. It may look like nothing, but it's not. My dad made it. His other skill. When he's not making things grow, he's making things work. The port-com he built me is as good as anything you can order. Maybe better. Holding it close to my chest, I pick my way across the room and sit down next to a wardrobe. If anyone wakes to go to the toilet, they won't spot me here. They won't walk past me either. The exit is on the opposite side of the room.

Even so, I tilt my head and listen. Silence. The gentle sounds of sleep don't seem to travel beyond the wardrobe. I rest the port-com on my lap and open the screen.

My fingers hover above the keys. I type a few commands to peel away the pages which direct you to write, shop, plan, fix. The pages everyone uses. Beneath those lie what I want. The plain screens with nothing but code. Which look like boring nonsense. To most people.

A column of numbers appears to the left. To the right, scrolls a mixture of words and symbols which make no sense at all. Light from the screen casts an eerie glow on my fingers. I scan the last few lines and begin to type. My eyes flick left and right, searching for a clue. A sequence. I begin to type again. Words and symbols dance through my head. They make sense to me.

I hear something. A noise which travels beyond the wardrobe. I push myself closer to the wall and lower my screen to hide the glow. Someone is moving. There is a rustle of sheets. I glance at my port-watch. I've been here for an hour. Normally I would stay twice as long, but I need some sleep.

The rustling stops, but I count to twenty. To be safe.

Slowly, I raise the screen, preparing to shut down, but as the letters and numbers glow once more in the darkness, I pause. I can't believe I didn't see it before. One line of the sequence is clearly wrong. The bug. The section of code with the error. Excitement buzzes in my chest.

I copy the line, then open my encrypted message service, clicking on the symbol of a small black beetle. JP's symbol. The one who set me the challenge. The hardest challenge they've thought up so far, and it only took me three days to figure out.

Record time? I write, then insert the piece of code.

They're probably asleep, so I'll just have to wait until tomorrow to find out if it's right.

And if it is right, I'll do a victory dance in my head. I can't tell anyone. Not Chloe or Finn. Nobody. JP is the only one who knows my secret, and I know theirs—because it's the same secret. In a world where everything is digital, we are something forbidden. Dangerous.

We are cyber-spies.

Hackers.

Retail

In my dream, Mum is checking Chloe's oxygen levels. The port-watch sounds an alarm, a *beep* which continues until I realize the noise is coming from elsewhere. Not my dream. I open my eyes and look around, trying to remember where I am—a room full of beds and people. The beeping fades, leaving a soft echo.

I rub my eyes. Someone yawns. It's time to get up. But no one seems to be moving.

I become aware of a new sound. A low buzzing.

'Drone!'

Instinctively, I look through the dim morning light towards Mae's bed, but she is lying down. I'm surprised to see that the voice belongs to Eve. With a few long strides she reaches the window in the centre of the room and presses the button to raise the blind. No one complains. Two or three other girls have gathered a safe distance nearby, watching. One of them with short brown hair, Nyla, I think, raises her port-watch to scan the drones. I assume to identify their serial numbers.

I don't need to look. I know there's nothing for me. I'm impressed that anyone has found time to shop. We've been here less than twenty-four hours.

'Four packages,' says Eve. 'No, wait, five!' She stretches up, to peer through the top corner of the window. Shrinking-Eve has morphed into a statuesque drone-spotter.

There is a new energy in the room.

When I turn round, Ana is already getting dressed. In her palm sits a small turquoise container which matches her luggage.

'What's in the box?' I ask, pulling on my socks.

'Monday health supplements,' she says.

'Monday?'

'They're different every day of the week. Aren't yours?'

'I don't take any,' I say.

Ana's eyes widen.

I can't be sure, but it feels as if she moves away from me, slightly.

'Don't you get ill all the time?'

'No,' I smile.

*

After breakfast we divide into subject groups. I follow the arrows to language studies, my heart thumping in my chest. I'm about to have my first lesson in a classroom—as if I'm stepping into one of Dad's old films.

When the door slides open, though, it's nothing like I'd imagined. The tables are arranged in a semi-circle rather than rows. But that's not what makes it weird. There are nine or ten kids already seated, and they are yelling at the teacher.

'I want to see it now.'

'What if it's damaged and I need to change it? I'll have to wait longer for a new one.'

'You can't stop me from getting my stuff.'

I freeze by the doorway, trying to work out what's going on.

The teacher sits calmly in her chair, waiting for them to stop.

After a few minutes, no one has anything new to add.

The teacher takes a slow breath in and out, and says, 'Thank you for your comments. I will share them with the principal. You should be aware that your parents were informed of the rules regarding in-school shopping.' I hear several intakes of breath. 'It's something we encourage families to discuss before the start of your first term. You may collect your items at the end of the school day. Not before.'

A few students roll their eyes, but no one speaks.

I move quietly towards an empty seat near the end of the semi-circle, between a boy and a girl from a different dormitory.

We tilt our heads for a better view of the giant screen behind the teacher, waiting for the lesson to begin.

I realize the teacher is watching us.

She smiles a weary looking smile, then adds, 'For this lesson there will be no screen. Just me.'

Therapy

I walk as quickly as I can, glancing now and then at the purple arrows on the wall. Only because they're distracting. I've learnt my way around.

The dormitory door slides open and I hurry inside. No one else is here. I'm grateful for even a few minutes to myself. I knew school would be nothing like home. I didn't realize there would be people who make no sense to me. I can't make sense of any of the other girls here, yet.

I lie on my bed for a few minutes and stare at the ceiling. Then I walk over to Dad's trunk. My trunk. Most of its contents have been stored in drawers or cupboards around the room. Nestled at the bottom, beneath my old grey jumper, are my most precious things. I peel back the jumper and breathe in the smell. A scent of paper and leather, mixed with something warm and familiar. Bibliosmia. Mum taught me that word. I thought it was something to do with the Bible, but it's from the ancient Greek words for 'book' and 'smell'. A smell that I love. The smell of books. Now it also reminds me of home. Dad has a huge collection of books. A library. After Mum, Chloe and me, Dad's books are what he treasures most. He lets me read whatever I want. A few days ago, he came into my room with a small box, gripping it tightly as if it were heavy, or precious, or both.

He placed it on the floor by my feet. 'Something to keep you busy during all that free time you won't have. I know you'll look after them,' he said.

I knelt and lifted the flaps. Inside, nestled side by side, were two neat stacks of books.

'But—' I tried to argue that they might get damaged or lost. But the truth is, as soon as Dad said I could take the books, I realized how much I wanted them. I was leaving home, but now a little part of it was coming with me. Stories for when I needed a hug. Stories which made me feel brave, or which made me laugh.

I'm not sure what I need right now, so I take a book from the top. The story of an orphan sent to live abroad with relatives she'd never met before, and the secret which sets her free. I've read it more times than I can remember.

I'm a few lines in, when the door opens. I carry on reading, wondering if whoever it is will notice I'm here.

Footsteps pad gently across the floor.

'Wow!'

I jump, almost dropping the book.

'Is that real?' Mae is at the foot of my bed, eyebrows raised. I stare at her for a few seconds, then realize she's talking about the book. 'I mean, is it an original?'

'It's my dad's. He collects them.'

'Can I have a look?'

I pass it to Mae, who takes it with both hands. She studies the front cover, then gently opens it to look inside.

She turns a few pages. 'They're so thin!' she says, smiling. 'Does it do anything?' When I don't answer, she looks up. 'You know, or is it just—pages?'

'It's just pages,' I say. Then I wonder what's wrong with *just* pages.

'I've never held one before. It's heavier than I thought it would be.'

'Much heavier than a screen,' I agree, 'and you can't switch it off or delete it. But I like that. It's always there. Even when you're sleeping.'

Mae flicks through a few more pages before handing it back. She hovers round the end of my bed. I'm not sure whether to carry on reading.

'You didn't say, yesterday, whether you'd ever met any kids for real, before coming here.'

'Oh,' I reply, trying to remember the conversation. 'I have a younger sister, Chloe. You have a sister too, don't you?'

'Yes, and I bet she's enjoying the extra space in our room.'

I feel as if Mae wants me to agree. I think about Chloe on the sofa when I left, her face pale, her eyes closed.

'I'm worried that mine is going to find it hard. Now that I've gone, and Finn has–' I stop myself before I say any more, but it's already too late.

'Who's Finn?' Mae asks.

Before I can answer, her port-watch beeps, and so does mine.

'Programming,' she says brightly.

But I can tell that her mind isn't entirely on our next lesson. She's wondering why I might have met other children, before coming to school.

Pretend

I seem to arrive a little late. All the seats are taken except one at the far end of the semi-circle. I can't see anyone from my dorm. No Mae. Everyone studies programming, so maybe they mix up the dorms on purpose, to make sure we spend time with other students.

There is a buzz in the room. For the first time since we arrived, the big screen is switched on. It's the hologram-interactive type we use at home for live-learning. I wonder why everyone is excited by something so familiar.

Smaller screens and keyboards emerge from the smooth surface of each desk. When the teacher sets a few warm-up questions, all I can hear is the gentle tapping of fingertips. It's hard not to be distracted by the green tick 'holograms' hovering over our heads with each correct answer.

'Now I'm going to start with a few trickier problems,' the teacher warns, sitting forwards in his chair. 'This isn't a test, it's just to help me work out what we need to focus on.' He smiles a warm smile which makes the corners of his eyes crinkle. I try to concentrate on my screen. I can tell the teacher is watching us. He said this wasn't a test, but it feels like one. Green ticks begin to multiply. The space above my desk is empty.

I can answer the questions. That's not the problem. I can solve these puzzles with my eyes shut, but I don't want to draw attention to myself. Not when it comes to coding and programming. Not until I see what everyone else can do. I start slowly, glancing at the big screen from time to time. A tally of answers appears next to a semi-circle plan of the desks. The 'Jess' desk has five green tally marks. As the problems get harder, I become less aware of the room around me. My fingers tap with a steady rhythm. I'm beginning to enjoy myself. As I enter my next answer, I realize that the room is quiet. I glance up at the big screen. Not only have I caught up, I am the first student to solve this problem. The only student.

'I think we'll stop there,' says the teacher. He smiles at me, then looks round the semi-circle. 'Shall we congratulate Jess on her answer? This was a tough challenge.'

He raises his hands and claps gently. No one joins in at first. They seem unsure what to do, then the boy next to me starts to clap, and a few others. I feel my face flush.

'Thank you,' I say, looking left to right.

I realize with surprise that there is someone from my dorm group here after all. It's the girl with black hair. She isn't clapping. She is scowling. She tries to rearrange her face into a smile, but it's too late. She's upset that I've beaten her. And I've done the opposite of what I wanted. Drawn attention to myself. I look up at the big screen and search for her desk on the plan. Her name is Violet.

Now that the not-a-test is over, a wave of tiredness washes over me. I half-hear the teacher say that he won't set any homework today. The lesson is almost over. I'm glad.

It's only Monday, but I am already thinking ahead to the weekend. We will be allowed time to speak to our families. I can't wait to see Chloe's face. To talk to Mum and Dad about real lessons.

Perhaps that will help me to figure out why school isn't what I expected. Nothing like the films.

Luck

My eyes flick open. The room is dark. There is something hard beneath my head. A quiet click from somewhere above me is followed by a soft humming sound. I hold my breath. Then let it go, slowly. I know that noise. The solar panels on the roof are moving to catch the morning sun. A sweet aroma hangs in the air, the scent of many different shampoos, from many sleeping heads. I remember where I am, but everything still feels so strange. Not the routine I know. Not the sounds and smells.

I lift a hand to my pillow, carefully sliding my port-com from under my left ear. I must have fallen asleep on it. I can't afford to be so careless. No one sleeps with their port-com under their pillow. I slide it towards the edge of the mattress. With my other hand I reach down and open the drawer. The port-com slips from my fingers and lands with a crack on the wooden edge. I gasp in shock. Ana sits up in her bed.

'What was that?' she says, staring around in confused half-sleep.

'Nothing,' I whisper, my heart pounding. 'Maybe someone knocking on the door.'

She lies back down.

Using my duvet as an anchor, I reach as far as I can, my fingers grazing the carpet. I grasp the edge of my port-com, lifting it into the drawer. It doesn't feel damaged. I just have to hope that nothing inside is broken.

I lie back down and notice a fine layer of sweat on my back, which has begun to cool. A pale rectangle of light filters beneath the blinds. I can't go back to sleep. Instead, my thoughts drift to my first ever hack.

I was looking for something to read. I remember browsing through Dad's bookshelves until I found a book with a strange title, something about lions and wardrobes. It sounded intriguing. As I slid it from the shelf, another book fell out. A thin, grey paperback. I took both to my room. Chloe lay on the bed next to me. I gave her the lion book and started flicking through the thin one. It used words I'd never heard of like 'binary', 'java', 'algorithm'. It talked about entire worlds made of code. That behind everything digital, were languages which computers can understand. Which you can use to instruct them, control them. I knew I had to learn one. Or as many as I could. The book said it could take years to be any good. It took me months. The more skilful I became, the more I wanted to use what I'd learnt. I wanted to test myself. Find out how good I really was. Near the back was a chapter called *Hero or Zero*. I had no idea—at first—but this was the chapter I needed.

It talked about people who were so good at programming that they could find mistakes in other people's code. They could save companies millions of pounds by discovering weak spots in their computer systems. 'Hackers'. Some people did it to help, some did it to cheat others out of money, or create chaos. Some did it for fun. But they all had one thing in common. They were the best.

That's what I wanted to be.

Live-learning taught us that cybercriminals were the most dangerous in the world, and the most hunted. That cybercrime could bring the world to an end, literally. Dad's book was written a long time ago, before everything was digital. Still, it talked about the risks of hacking.

Perhaps that should have put me off. But I was desperate to use my knowledge. To use my skills.

I decided to try eavesdropping. A passive hack, where you simply observe and monitor. You're not actually *doing* anything. Much. But the system I was 'sniffing' information from alerted another hacker. As soon as I'd gained access, they began eavesdropping—on me. The next day I received a note on my port-watch, directing me to an encrypted messaging service.

Instead of handing me over, the hacker told me what I'd done wrong. That I should be more careful. That the best way to get really good was to have a hacking 'buddy'. To set challenges for each other. Bugs to find, systems to crack. They wanted a hacking buddy to practise with, before trying stuff out for real. I lacked finesse, but I had potential. They were willing to give me a chance. What did I think? Since they already knew my secret, I realized I had nothing to lose. If they'd wanted to hand me over to the police, they could have done so already. Perhaps I had something to gain.

So I guess my first hack was my worst, but also my luckiest.

Since then, we've messaged every day, with ideas, questions, problems to solve. Until yesterday. For the first time in two years, I didn't get in touch.

I hope JP doesn't mind. I'm the one who never makes mistakes, now. The one who comes up with the best short cuts and software. I don't want JP to think I don't need them any more. I suspect upsetting another hacker would be a bad idea.

Ana stirs again. It must nearly be time for the wake-up bell. I close my eyes, then open them again. If I fall asleep now, I know I will feel far worse. At least my first lesson is also the one I've been looking forward to most. Music.

We wait in silence. There are only six of us, seated in a cluster near the centre of a huge room, not much smaller than the dining hall. I am trying to work out which instruments the other students play from the shape of their cases, when a small woman in a bright pink dress appears in the doorway.

'I'm so sorry I'm late,' she says, rushing to join us. 'I'm Miss Singer.'

I smile. There are a few stifled giggles from the other students.

'Yes, I know. It's a silly name for a music teacher. But we don't get to choose our names.' She tucks a stray piece of hair behind her ear as another one falls across her face.

I feel my grip on the violin case begin to loosen, but the knot in my stomach remains. I've only ever played for *real* in front of my family before.

'Now,' says Miss Singer, laying her port-com on the floor next to her chair, 'we're mostly going to get to know each other today. We only start performing symphonies in week two.' She smiles. 'Jessica.'

I look at her in surprise. She knows my name.

'Jessica, perhaps you could start by telling us about your favourite pudding.'

I hear myself laughing, and realize, with a small spark of happiness, that Miss Singer might be someone who makes sense to me.

Accident

The next few days are so busy, I barely have time to think about home. Some afternoon clubs have started, so I sign up for chess, wondering if it might be a good way to meet people. There is only one other boy at my first session. I already know how to play, but he doesn't, so the teacher spends most of his time explaining how to set up the board and what the different pieces do. The boy keeps asking whether that's *all* they do. I'm not sure he'll come back next week, which means it will be just me and the teacher.

I haven't had time for my port-com, either. I guess it's not that I haven't had time. Every night is a chance to message JP, but I can't seem to stay awake. I can't risk setting an alarm either, without waking someone else. JP must be wondering what's happened to me.

On Friday, Mae and I are both free, so we wander back to the common room together.

'What's your ROOM like?' Mae's voice seems strangely loud in the corridor. No one talks much between lessons.

'You mean my virtual ROOM?' I ask, then feel stupid. That's the only 'room' people mean.

'Yes,' she smiles. 'Only, I don't see you scanning much.'

'I never really buy anything new to share in it.' I don't want to tell Mae that we have no spare credits. That Mum and Dad try to live without screens as much as possible. 'I haven't seen you scanning either.'

Mae stops walking. She looks up and down the corridor dramatically, before whispering, 'I find it boring.' I raise my eyebrows in surprise. 'Really. I do. And it probably *is* best not to share that,' she adds.

'Your secret is safe with me,' I whisper back.

We pass through the door to the common room, when Mae says, 'Can I see the rest of your books?'

I don't remember telling Mae I had others, but hear myself replying, 'Of course. There are quite a few.'

I feel a strange flutter in my stomach, and I'm not sure why. I'm pleased that Mae is interested. Perhaps a little part of me wants to ask Dad whether he minds. Even though I know he wouldn't.

As we walk over to my trunk, I see Ana lying on her bed wearing a pair of VR glasses, a holographic tiger cub curled at her feet. She doesn't stir. I guess she hasn't noticed we're here. I see that she has port-buds in her ears, too. She could be in space, or the desert or under the sea right now. Wherever her glasses have taken her.

'It looks so old,' Mae says, tapping the top of the trunk with her finger, as if it might be a hologram too. 'Is it really as old as it looks?'

'I think so. It used to be my dad's. My grandad made it for him.'

'Amazing,' she adds.

The grey-blue sides are girdled with strips of copper-coloured wood and edged with black metal. It looks as if it could gobble up the other furniture in the room.

I lift the heavy lid and push the grey jumper aside. Mae's eyes sparkle as I place a small pile of books on the bed.

'What's a compendium?' she asks. 'Here's the orphan one again.' She picks up another. 'I love the silvery cover! Why do some of them have hard covers and some of them have bendy covers?'

'Dad says you could buy hardback books or paperback books. People usually bought hardback books as presents.'

'You'd need strong arms to read this one in bed,' she smiles, balancing a thick book with a blue cover in the palm of her hand. 'It would knock you out if you dropped it.'

'Are you going to the S1 Ice Breaker?' says a voice softly.

Mae and I jump.

Violet is standing near the end of the bed. Her eyes rest briefly on my face, then the books, before resting on my face again.

I'm not sure how long she's been standing there.

A lock of black hair falls across her cheek, and she brushes it away, without blinking.

I glance at my port-watch.

'Oh no! I'd completely forgotten about it. We're going to be late. Thank you for reminding us, Violet,' I add. I feel as if I'm constantly heading somewhere, and always late. 'You two go ahead and I'll catch you up.'

'I can help you put the books back,' says Mae. Before I answer, she scoops up five or six from the bed and carries them towards the trunk. As she leans over, one slides from the top and hits the back of the trunk with a cracking thump. She gasps.

I leap up, taking the rest of the pile from her and placing it carefully on the bed.

'I'm so sorry, Jess!' says Mae.

Tears sting my eyes as I reach in to retrieve the hardback with the blue cover. I can see that one of the corners is completely squashed.

'Can't you buy a new one?' asks Violet.

I shake my head. 'Not any more.'

Mae puts her fingertips to her lips, her eyes wide. 'Oh, Jess, I think I've damaged your trunk, too.'

I turn back to the trunk. There is a blue line running down the back, a trail left by the book, slicing through the ornate name plate pasted inside.

'We're going to be late,' says Violet.

Mae hesitates.

'I'll join you in a minute,' I say, my voice as steady as I can make it.

'OK. See you there. Sorry,' says Mae.

'I think you've done her a favour,' I hear Violet say, 'now she can get something better.'

They are halfway across the room, but I'm sure she meant me to hear.

I wait for the door to close behind them before a sob shakes my shoulders.

In the space of a few seconds, I've damaged two things which Dad trusted me to look after. Two precious things.

A tear spills down my cheek. I don't want to leave water marks on the books too, so I dry my eyes on the sleeve of my jumper, then bend down to look more closely at the trunk.

The tiger cub on Ana's bed stretches and licks a paw, but Ana doesn't move. She still doesn't know I'm here.

Gently, I try to smooth the damaged edges of the name plate. They are so brittle that pieces flake off on my fingers. I'm about to put the books back, when I see something beneath the old fragments of paper. Gripping the edge of the trunk, I lean a little closer. It looks like writing.

Another piece of the name plate crumbles away. It will be impossible to fix. Dad might be more likely to notice a damaged label than no label, so I lift a corner of the paper to read what's written beneath. With a soft crackling noise, the rest comes away in one giant flake.

I stare at the oblong of slightly darker paint it has revealed. Neat black letters spell *Charlie Scott*.

Which is strange. Because that's not my dad's name.

Secret 3

I scan the room. Every chair is taken. Holograms flicker into life. Parents appear then disappear until adjusted. They tilt sideways or hover until fine-tuning allows them to rest comfortably in their chairs. Or at least appear to rest comfortably. The common room, normally so quiet, buzzes with noise.

It's Saturday afternoon. I've been looking forward to it since I first arrived—looking forward to Kin Space. Dad said why don't they just call it Family Time, instead of giving it a silly name. But right now I don't care. During the first week, you're supposed to focus on school. There's so much to take in. We're not allowed to get in touch with family. It's the one thing everyone seems to have been waiting for. I haven't even thought about our first team sports session afterwards, even though Chloe and I have spent years watching videos of hockey, football and netball, imagining what it might be like to play.

I'm desperate to see Chloe's face. To hear that she's had a good week. But there's another feeling, not completely obscured by my excitement: guilt. I feel bad about Dad's book and his trunk. Guilty that he trusted me to look after them and I haven't.

Fragments of conversation hum through the air. Ana holds up something to show her parents. They are squashed onto one seat, arms and shoulders overlapped, creating a strange fuzzy effect. They smile and nod as she speaks. Violet sits quietly opposite her mother, who is talking in a low, serious voice.

I spot a table by the window. That will do. I don't need extra chairs for holograms, just somewhere to balance my port-com.

I sense the seconds ticking away, even though Kin Space lasts a whole hour.

My port-com vibrates. When I lift the screen, Finn's face appears.

'Jess! Were you waiting for me to connect?' he grins.

I don't have the heart to tell him I was about to connect home.

My grin mirrors his, though.

'I've barely moved from here,' I say. 'Just waiting. People have to bring me food.'

'I've met all the live-learning guys,' says Finn. 'Jack is a lot taller than he looks on the screen. It's really weird. I think his imager must have been at the wrong angle for the last eight years. What about your school? What's everyone like?'

Even though I've been looking forward to seeing Finn all week, for some reason, I can't think of anything I want to share. I'm not used to seeing him on a screen. An image of the bent book keeps floating into my head. I know Finn would make me feel better about it, but he seems so excited, so happy, I don't want to mention it.

'There's no one here from live-learning, but everyone seems nice.' I never use the word 'nice'. 'The music classes are really good.'

'Tell Chloe I'm waiting for a message from her,' he adds. 'I thought she might have sent one by now. I bet your mum and dad are keeping her busy—since you've abandoned her.'

I feel my grin fading. I try to lift the corners of my mouth back into a smile.

'Actually, she's written hundreds to me. Perhaps she just doesn't like you any more.'

I hear someone else's voice. Finn turns his head. When he turns back, he is smiling again.

'Jess, I have to go. We've got football now. Real football!'

'Good luck! I hope you manage to kick something.' I wave, and the screen goes dark.

I'm about to connect to Mum and Dad, when my port-com vibrates again and they appear, perched on the old blue sofa. Chloe is sandwiched in the middle, snuggled in a blanket of bright, knitted squares, just like when I saw her last.

'Jessy-loo!' she squeals. 'Can you show us around? I want to see your bedroom.'

'Let's find out how she is first,' says Mum, 'then if there's time, she can show us.'

'But what if there *isn't* time?'

'I'm still here,' I wave.

'You look well,' Dad chips in, 'maybe a little tired.'

'How are the goats? Are they missing me?' I ask. Seeing them all, nestled on the sofa, fills me with an overwhelming desire to be there too.

'We all are,' says Mum.

'I am,' says Chloe. 'Although I do get to lie on the top bunk to read.'

Chloe seems fine, but then she usually does. Her cheeks are pale.

As if reading my mind, Mum says, 'Chloe has had a tough week, haven't you, Chlo?' She nods. 'We've got through quite a lot of medicine.'

'I haven't been back to the treehouse. Mum's going

down there later to get my package from Finn. I gave her special one-day Treehouse Membership.'

'Good. He's waiting for a message from you.'

Chloe grins. I notice a pair of brown pointy ears poking out from the side of the blanket. Chloe hugs the blanket towards her. There is a soft mewing sound. I know that Mum and Dad have heard it too, but they don't react.

We chat about how many orders for honey Mum has taken, and the late harvest. I tell Chloe about lessons in an actual classroom, with a teacher in front of you. She listens wide-eyed.

It almost begins to feel like being at home. But there is no baked-bread smell wafting from the warm kitchen. No hugs.

I realize the hour is nearly up.

'Have you had any time for reading?' asks Dad. I feel a hollow sensation in my stomach as I think of the book and the crushed corner.

'I—not much, they make sure you're pretty busy.' I'm about to change the subject when I remember the trunk. I have a sudden impulse to find out whose name was beneath the label. But if I ask Dad, I might have to tell him about dropping the book. I hesitate, but curiosity gets the better of me. 'Dad, who is Charlie Scott?'

My dad seems to recoil from the screen. He and Mum exchange a glance.

'Where did you hear that name?' Dad's voice is barely a whisper. His face is ashen.

Chloe looks up at him, frowning.

'It's written in your trunk. Beneath the label with your name on.'

He closes his eyes.

When he opens them again, he doesn't look like Dad. There is no twinkle in his eye. His expression is rigid, fixed.

'Jess.' Even though he is speaking softly, I can hear the urgency in his tone. 'It would be best if you didn't mention that name to anyone else.' I nod slowly. 'Perhaps don't let anyone see inside your trunk, either.'

I nod again. Every other part of me seems to have frozen.

Dad relaxes a little. 'You can bring it home with you at half term. Then we can fix it.'

His tone has changed from dark-mystery to small-DIY-project in the space of a few seconds. Perhaps he realized he was starting to scare me.

Chloe is looking from Mum to Dad, trying to work out what's happening.

Mum wraps an arm tightly around her shoulders. 'When can we do this again?'

'We're allowed Kin Space every day now, but it has to be at this time. Sometimes I have extra classes.'

'No problem,' says Mum. 'We'll bring one of the goats to say hi next time, too.'

She seems to be trying hard to sound casual. Cheerful. I try too, for Chloe.

'I'll be waiting for a message, Chlo. And I'll be really upset if you send one to Finn and not me.'

She smiles. 'OK. As soon as they let me do anything.' She rolls her eyes towards Mum and Dad.

We wave to each other. The screen goes dark. For a few moments, I don't move.

Then I become aware that the common room is completely quiet.

I look up, as the last students are leaving. I'm just about to follow, when I spot Mae, a few seats away. She is leaning back, staring at the ceiling. I don't remember seeing her earlier. I wonder how long she's been there. How much she heard. She looks over.

'Finally! I was about to give up on you,' she says. 'Which sport are you doing?'

I pause, trying to remember. My mind is still caught up in the conversation with Dad.

'I think I signed up for hockey.'

'Me too. Let's go together.' She jumps up and heads for the dorm. I follow more slowly. I want a few moments to run through what just happened, and why Dad was acting so strangely. A few moments to myself.

As I dawdle by the door, I notice movement out of the corner of my eye. There is someone else in the common room. Someone wearing trainers like Violet's.

'It's so far!' Nyla frowns at the hockey pitch, clutching the brand-new silver and red stick which I saw her scanning before breakfast this morning. Ana is placing one foot gently inside a bright blue trainer. When she slips her heel inside, the fabric shrinks, hugging the contours of her foot. I've heard of Skin Boots, but I've never seen them. I have Mum's hockey stick. She said that if I enjoyed playing, she would buy me a new one.

The pitch is no bigger than our apiary. Smaller than the meadow beyond. I've run up and down both hundreds of times.

'The pitches look smaller on my VR glasses,' Nyla adds gloomily.

The teacher walks over, placing a container of hockey sticks by her feet, but we all have our own. Perhaps that explains the drone activity yesterday morning.

'Right, has anyone played before?' she asks.

Almost everyone puts their hands up. I know they mean VR hockey. 'Excellent! Let's get warmed up.'

Several girls produce pills from capsules on their wrists.

'May I remind you that healthplan supplements are not to be taken just before or during sports,' says the teacher sternly.

'But they're part of my healthplan for sports. When else can I take them?' says a tall girl I always see in the dining hall.

'This rule is applied at all schools, for your own safety. We don't want any choking incidents.'

The tall girl puts a hand to her neck, looking shocked, but takes her pills once the teacher turns away.

We are split into pairs to practise ball skills. Mae partners with me, and we run down the field, passing back and forth. After five minutes or so, some girls stop what they're doing and lean on their sticks. A few are sitting on the ground.

'You're really good,' I say to Mae, as we dribble the ball round some cones. Did you have the VR game at home?' She doesn't answer.

Soon we are the only ones on our feet.

The teacher doesn't seem surprised. She beckons us

over. The others stand up wearily, checking the heart monitors on their port-watches.

'Well done, everyone,' she says. 'You might find playing sport outside slightly different to VR. It's normal to feel more tired. You may wish to speak to your parents about adjusting your supplement regime.'

A few girls nod their heads. One or two of them sniff and rub their eyes.

I want to say I feel the same. That I wish hockey was over, and it's better in VR. But I don't. I sit in silence with them. Instead of worrying about supplements, I'm worrying about how I will stay awake tonight. I *have* to message JP.

JP

I lie still, listening. As usual the room is silent. Dusky moonlight sneaks beneath the edges of the blind. The only witness as I creep across the room to my corner beside the wardrobe. Before lifting the lid to my port-com, I sit for a minute, thinking about Mum and Dad. Their shocked expressions earlier. That Dad had seemed almost–frightened.

I have four encrypted messages from JP.

I read them quickly. I need to know that things are OK.

The first one says:

Not quite record time. Close.

It doesn't take me long to read the rest.

Got a challenge for me?

Problems? Let me know.

Will wait to hear.

JP doesn't sound upset.

I feel my shoulders relax and realize that my whole body was tense.

I begin to type. I know exactly what my new challenge will be. I've had six days to think about it. But this challenge has been on my mind for a long time.

I want to see how quickly JP can access a top security system and create a back door—a way to easily revisit without the need to hack from scratch.

I type the name of the system I have in mind. It belongs to the company which makes Chloe's medicine.

I'm about to carry on with a hack of my own, but I can't focus. The thoughts racing round my head all lead back to one thing: Charlie Scott. I know that Grandad made Dad's trunk, so he must have painted the name. Or did someone add it later? If so, who? Why was Dad so shocked when I mentioned it? It's just a name. Instead of finding answers, my questions seem to multiply.

On my port-watch, I type *Charlie Scott*. Lots of results appear. I don't know how to narrow my search, without knowing anything about the person I'm searching for. I type *Charlie Scott* and *mystery*. A few random things appear. I suppose it's only a mystery for me. I type in *Charlie Scott bad*, then *Charlie Scott criminal*. There are still too many results to trawl through. Anyway, how would I know if I'd found anything relevant?

I breathe out slowly. I don't like problems I can't solve.

I go back to my encrypted messages and begin to type. My chest feels tight. I'm about to do something I've never done before: ask JP a question which has nothing to do with hacking.

If I need to research someone, where do I start?

I don't expect a reply. JP normally takes a day or two. But a message appears in my account immediately.

It's not me, is it?

I reply: *Never.*

A new message appears.

Government database. Register of births/deaths. No need to hack. There could be hundreds.

The information I need is available to everyone. Not secret at all. I feel deflated. Stupid for asking.

OK. Thank you.

Finding the registry takes a few seconds. I feel my eyelids drooping. I need to sleep.

There is only one page of 'Charlie Scott's for the last one hundred years, nowhere near as many as I thought. There are dates for when they were born, married, and when they died, but nothing else. With no clues, no other information, I'm stuck again. I close up my port-com.

I guess I'll just have to be patient and talk to Dad during half term.

Even though I waited so long to start school, I know that the next six weeks will feel like for ever.

Jack

My port-watch buzzes. I glance down but keep on walking. I don't want to be late for music.

P6h edvzh sc zc 2vvh dteh w6brh f4f w8h rtzzc 78 c84 rtjv f67w6brh 2vtehe? F6ee c84 l kk

I blink and look again. For a few seconds I am confused. Then I realize the message is from Chloe. I smile. She's used Finn's secret code. I see, also, the irony of not being able to understand what she's written. It is secret from me too, until I have a few moments to myself, which won't be until this afternoon.

I raise my head, just in time to swerve out of Miss Fischer's way.

'Jessica, port-watches on sleep mode until lunchtime. You know that.'

'Sorry, Miss Fischer,' I reply, a glow of frustration in

my chest. I hardly ever check my port-watch, unlike everyone else. Never in her science class.

When I walk into the music room, instead of five students I count six. A new boy has joined our group. One I don't recognize from other lessons or from mealtimes. Beside his chair is a violin case. At least, I think that's what it is. It looks nothing like mine, but then most things here look nothing like mine. It's completely smooth, with a gentle curve near the middle, to tuck beneath your arm.

Miss Singer waits for me to sit down. Our small cluster of chairs still seems lost in the large, high-ceilinged room.

'Please say hello to Jack,' she smiles. 'Jack wasn't well enough to join us at the start of term, but I'm sure you will make him feel welcome.'

The other students exchange worried looks. They don't want to catch whatever Jack had. Even though they know that Jack would never be allowed back to school if he were contagious. Jack is focussing on the floor a few metres from his chair. I smile at the side of his head. He glances up, and a smile twitches one corner of his mouth.

We warm up by playing scales together. Two of the class play the flute, one piano, and another two the guitar. I was the only violinist, until now. I notice that

Jack's violin is carved from a sleek, black wood. It's beautiful. Even though we are only practising scales, the notes he plays are pure and clear.

'Has anyone finished their composition?' Miss Singer asks.

No one puts their hands up. She set the task at the end of our last lesson. She said we could take two weeks to work on it. Slowly, I raise mine.

'Well done, Jessica. Would you like to play it for us?'

I hesitate. I've rehearsed the notes in my head, but I haven't yet played them on my violin.

'I'll play it,' says a soft voice.

I look round, and realize the voice belongs to Jack.

'If you're happy, Jessica?' says Miss Singer.

I nod.

She passes Jack a music stand. As the screen unfurls, they look at me expectantly.

'Oh! Sorry.' I realize that they're waiting for my music. Rather than tapping my port-watch on the stand, I pull a crumpled square of paper from my pocket. I know it's easier to use port devices. I just prefer paper. I think more carefully about how the notes will sound when I write them down.

Jack tries to smooth out the creases, then rests the page on the edge of the stand. It slips down, ending up at a gentle tilt.

He stares at the music for a minute or so, then lifts his bow.

The notes are pitch-perfect, the pace and phrasing are exactly how I imagined. As if he can hear the melody playing inside my head.

He finishes with a flourish. For a second I wonder whether he might take a bow. Then, as if a switch has flicked, he sits down quietly in his chair, resting his violin on his knees.

Miss Singer stands very still, looking towards the spot where Jack stood seconds before. Her head begins to nod, as if to an echo of the music.

I wonder why she's taking so long to comment. I don't see how she can fault Jack's playing, so it must be my composition. I'm beginning to wish I hadn't put my hand up. No one else did. I could have taken more time to work on it, like the others. I feel as if I've shared something private, something which wasn't ready.

'Jack, your playing is sublime,' Miss Singer says eventually. Then she turns to me. 'Jessica, who taught you to write music?'

'I—no one.'

Miss Singer doesn't move. She seems to be waiting for more.

'I taught myself.'

She keeps staring, as if I've just sprouted horns, or something equally ridiculous.

'I watched some tutorials. I listened to a lot of violin music too.' I can't seem to stop talking. I wish Miss Singer would say something. The other students start shifting in their chairs.

She blinks a few times, as if waking from a trance. 'You didn't give Jack one of the pieces you've been learning at home? By accident,' she adds hastily.

'No,' I say, feeling confused.

'Well, it was very–impressive,' she says, almost to herself. 'The melody–the nuance.' She smiles round the room, as if inviting the others to agree.

'I really liked it,' says one of the flautists, smiling.

My cheeks burn. A strange feeling of lightness has come over me. It's the same feeling I have when I solve one of JP's challenges. When I unravel a difficult hack. Only this is something I can share with more than one person. It doesn't have to be a secret.

We continue the lesson, everyone taking it in turns to play. Towards the end, Miss Singer taps her port-com to share the piece of music we'll be learning to play ensemble.

As we put our instruments away, she says, 'Thank you, everyone. Jack and Jessica, could you please stay behind.'

Miss Singer waits for the door to close, then sits in silence for a few seconds, clutching her port-com.

'I've been teaching for a long time,' she says, 'and I've never had a lesson like today's. I feel as if I've stumbled on some magic, this afternoon. I knew about your playing,' she smiles at Jack, 'I've listened to your live-learning recordings.' She turns to me. There is an energy in her eyes, a spark. 'But I had no idea about your composition skills, Jessica. Did you work on that piece for long?'

The melody had been floating in my head for a few weeks, but it didn't take me long to write down.

'Mostly over the weekend,' I say.

Musical notes feel strangely like writing code. Part language, part puzzle. There are different paths, different solutions, but one of them is always best.

She nods eagerly. 'I feel there is wonderful potential here. With the right guidance—' She pauses, as if struggling to find the right words. 'Would you,' she hesitates, 'would you be happy to have some extra tuition? I'm afraid it would only be once a week. After lesson time.'

Miss Singer looks first at me, then Jack. I think about how little time I have already. Then I remember the strange lightness I felt earlier.

I nod my head. Jack is looking at me.

'Yes, me too,' he says.

'Excellent!' Miss Singer beams. 'I'll have a look at my schedule and see when we might fit something in.'

Jack and I walk down the corridor together. It's empty. Everyone else is having lunch.

'Do you know your way around?' I ask. Jack is only just keeping up. I remember that he's been ill and slow down a little.

'I think so. But if in doubt, follow the arrows?' He smiles.

'Well, I'm going to put my violin away. The dining hall is that way, then right,' I point vaguely down the corridor. 'Just in case you can't find an arrow.'

'OK,' he says. He looks pale. I realize that his voice has a slight wheeze. Like Chloe's.

When I arrive a few minutes later, Jack is near the front of the queue talking to another S1 boy. I'm glad that he has made a friend already.

I go over to sit with Mae. Although our classes are mixed, most of S1 still seem to eat in their dorm groups.

'I thought you weren't coming,' says Mae.

There is a rattle of containers as Violet and Nyla dispense their lunchtime health supplements.

'The music teacher kept me behind.'

'Ooh what did you do?' Mae asks, eyes shining with excitement.

'She liked my composition.'

'Oh. Well, I guess that's good.'

I smile. 'There was a new boy in the class. He played the piece I'd written. He was amazing.'

'Where is he?' Mae whispers conspiratorially.

I nod my head towards his table. 'Over there. Black hair.' I feel my cheeks flush, and Mae notices. They burn even hotter.

'He looks very—*musical,*' she grins.

I laugh and choke on the water I'm sipping.

A few people glance over. Perhaps they are worried I might be coming down with something.

The neat-bot trundles past and I place our trays in one of the empty slots, before it sets off round the hall again.

'Let's go to the field,' Mae suggests.

'OK.' I really want some fresh air. We head out of the dining hall, straight into a crowd gathered in the corridor.

'Get the teacher!' someone yells. 'We need help.'

I can't see what's wrong, but no one is moving—or helping. The crowd isn't big, but people have backed away from whatever is at the centre. I stand on my tiptoes. It's Jack. He's propped against the wall. His face is pale and his breath is coming in short wheezes.

I push through the other students and crouch next to him. He lifts his hand weakly. A round container sits in his palm. I take it from his hand and flip open the lid. Inside lies a small pump and mask. Attached to the mask is a vial of medicine. Exactly the same as Chloe's. I know what to do. I place the mask over Jack's mouth and nose, making sure there are no gaps, then I press the pump. I count to sixty and press it again.

'Move aside!' A woman's voice rings out. 'Please go outside, or to your common rooms. Now!'

The group thins as students move away. I see one boy lift his port-watch to scan Jack, slumped against the wall.

A nurse from the health centre appears beside me. She clips an oximeter to Jack's finger.

'I gave him two puffs,' I say.

'Well done,' she says briskly. 'Was he able to tell you what he needed?'

'I knew what to do.'

She opens her mouth to say something, but at that moment a stretcher glides past, lowering itself gently to the floor next to Jack. A second nurse arrives.

While they are busy making Jack comfortable, I head outside to join Mae.

It takes me a while to spot her. She is sitting halfway across the field near a large oak tree, waving madly.

I pass a group of students on their port-watches. One of them scans me surreptitiously.

I walk quickly, my feet swishing against the grass. I like being surrounded by green. It reminds me of the meadow at home.

'You were amazing,' Mae calls before I reach her. 'I had no idea what was going on. It's like you saved his life or something.'

'I didn't save his life.'

'Well, he didn't look good. Is it catching?'

'No.'

'But how do you know? And how did you know what to do?'

I pause. 'My sister uses the same medication.'

Mae looks at me, her mouth drops open very slightly. 'Oh, I didn't know.'

I shrug. 'She's OK. The medication really helps.' I think back to the container in Jack's hand. There were three unopened vials of medicine–enough to last Chloe several months.

'My mum taught a little boy who–' Mae stops and looks up at me quickly.

'Your mum's a teacher?' I ask, raising my eyebrows.

Mae nods slowly.

'Wow. That's cool.'

Mae is quiet.

…he doesn't teach here, does she?'

…, not here.'

I pick at a blade of grass. For some reason, I feel as if I have upset her, but I don't know how. I'm about to change the subject, when Mae says, 'My mum teaches in a school, but not like this one.'

'She's a live-learning teacher?'

'No.'

I frown. There aren't any other places you can teach. I feel like I'm missing something obvious. Something important.

'But you said she doesn't teach in a school like this one?'

'She teaches kids who don't want to live-learn. She has her own school.'

I stare at her.

'But—how? It's illegal to mix with other children before you're fourteen.' So it must be illegal to run a school. I don't say so, but Mae clearly thinks that's what I mean.

She looks at me, green eyes flashing, then gets to her feet. 'They're going in.'

'What?'

She brushes down her leggings and starts walking back across the field.

'But—what did I say?' I run to catch up with her.

'I thought you were different to the rest of them. Open-minded,' she says, walking so quickly that I have to jog to keep up.

'Mae, I don't understand,' I pant, slightly out of breath. 'Explain first, then you can judge me.' We're nearly back at the yard now, where the final few students are filtering through the door.

'I'll think about it,' she says.

Challenge

I unfold the piece of paper with Finn's code.

I feel guilty that I haven't found time to decipher Chloe's message until now. Ana is busy on her port-watch. The other girls are all getting ready for bed or heading to the washroom. No one is paying any attention to what I'm doing.

I write down the letters, but the message doesn't make sense until I split them into words. The first three are k-i-t so I know it must be cat related, which helps.

Kit slept by my feet last night. Mum not happy. Do you have midnight feasts? Miss you, C *xx*

I feel a warm tingle in my chest. I like the idea of Kit keeping Chloe company when I'm not there.

Letter by letter, I transfer my reply into code:

F67w6brh 2vtehe vjvac w6brh. Fc sv7 6e 24dd 82 la4fse. L84d7 78 96hr P6h rvav h8 vth hrvf 4z. B6jv rva t h6lpdv svr6w7 hrv vtae 2a8f fv kk N

Midnight feasts every night. My bed is full of crumbs. Could do with Kit here to eat them up. Give her a tickle behind the ears from me xx J

Mae is perched on the edge of her bed, brushing her hair. She doesn't look my way.

Later, I check my messages from JP. Perhaps I've got used to being at school, or maybe I've caught up on some sleep, but I'm finding it easier to stay awake. JP hasn't mentioned my 'research' question from Saturday. I'm relieved because I'm not sure how I could explain it without sounding weird. I click on the black beetle and stare at the screen.

Challenge complete. Look.

I read the message again. How did JP find a solution so quickly? I'm impressed. The challenge was complicated.

I scan through how they accessed the system, then created a back door, allowing us to revisit the same areas whilst avoiding detection.

The methods JP used are elegant and concise. I shouldn't be surprised. I've never set a challenge JP couldn't solve—eventually. But there's just something about the speed and precision this time, which feels different. It's almost as if they've done it before.

Once I've placed my port-com safely in the drawer, my eyes drift shut. A melody weaves back and forth in my head. The notes melting into each other, perfectly pitched. Half awake, half asleep, I realize that it's the same clear sound as Jack's violin. The quavers twist into a line of code from JP's hack, floating ribbon-like through my sleepy mind. Somewhere, deep within my thoughts, an idea begins to form.

The next day I try to find a chance to talk to Mae. I need to know what she meant. But we only have one lesson together, and at lunchtime she has almost finished eating as I arrive. I feel like she will only talk to me when she's ready. If at all.

I spot Jack across the dining hall with some boys from his dorm. He looks a little better. Miss Singer has scheduled a private tuition session for Friday. He glances over and I feel my hand rise in a sort of half wave.

When lessons finish, Mae still isn't around, so I decide to call home. I need to have a normal chat about goats and carrots and what Chloe's been up to. I collect my port-com, side-stepping several tiger cubs which are roaming across the floor sniffing at the beds and furniture. It seems Ana has started a trend in our dormitory.

I send Mum a message on my port-watch, then rest my port-com on a table in the corner of the common room and wait. Several others drift in, arranging furniture to fit their hologram groups. Now we are allowed to call every day, Kin Space is less busy.

Violet adjusts a chair beneath a woman with the same black hair and dark blue eyes. She is chatting in a way I never see her talk to anyone here. She doesn't look bored. She even smiles, once.

My screen vibrates.

'Jessica-ca-ca!' Chloe sings. She is wrapped in a large woolly cardigan, sitting in a corner of the yard which catches the low afternoon sun. It casts a golden glow across her face.

'Are you having another midnight feast tonight?' she asks.

'Shhh, the teachers might hear.'

I can tell she's not entirely sure whether I'm teasing. She changes the subject anyway.

'I've been learning how to knit.' She smiles. 'Mum's teaching me how to make knitted animals. I might have a cat-shaped surprise for you.'

'Really?'

Two figures squash in on either side of Chloe.

'Her knitting's very good,' says Mum. She is clutching a ball of greeny-blue wool. Which means someone will be getting a new jumper or scarf, or both. 'It's nothing to do with this,' Mum adds, waving the wool at me. 'I'm making you a new jumper.'

I smile.

'It's going to be colder in the evenings soon.' She pauses. 'I'm not sure you will have a new coat this autumn. Chloe's medicine has gone up again.'

I frown. 'I thought it had already gone up—just before I started school.'

'It did. And a few months before that too.'

'There's not much we can do about it,' Dad chips in. 'We'll just have to concentrate on winter produce, once we've sold the autumn harvest.'

Dad rubs his chin. Something he normally does when the pancakes burn, or one of the goats escapes.

'What's the news, Jess?' he asks, his voice a little lighter. 'Chloe mentioned midnight feasts.'

'Lies,' I say. 'But I do have some news.' All three of them lean a little closer, even though I know they can hear me just fine. 'My music teacher, Miss Singer—'

'Did you say Miss "Singer"?' asks Dad.

'Yes. She really is called Miss Singer.'

Chloe giggles.

'She loved my composition piece so much that she's going to give me extra tuition.' Mum and Dad exchange a look. 'For free,' I add.

'That's amazing, Jess!' says Mum. 'Will you play it for us?'

'Aw, pleeease!' says Chloe.

'Maybe next time. Or I'll record myself. I've nearly finished a second piece, too.'

We chat about lessons and what Chloe has done in live-learning. No one mentions whether she's had any more serious episodes. I notice that when Dad smiles it doesn't quite reach his eyes, even when a chicken decides to wander in front of the screen.

When we say goodbye, a familiar empty feeling creeps over me. I wonder if Finn is around. I sent him a message too.

I lean back in my chair and listen to the gentle buzz of conversation around me. I wish the common room always felt like this.

'Helloooo!' My eyes flick back to the screen. Finn is waving frantically. I lean forwards so that I can hear him above the chatter, then I realize the voices are at his end.

'Is there some kind of party going on? I can hear lots of giggling.'

'If only,' he says. 'We didn't have any homework for the first week, but now we have *loads*. That's the sound of panic. How are you doing?'

'Not too bad. I've got extra music. The teacher–'

Finn has turned away from the screen. A few seconds later he turns back.

'Jess, I'm really sorry. It's break time and if I don't get to the common room fast enough there'll be nothing left.' He waves and gives me a big grin.

I wave back, just after the screen goes dark.

Puzzle

I know that Mae is avoiding me. After a few days I realize it's not just the mystery of her mother's school that I'm desperate to talk about. I want to tell Mae about Chloe, too. How the price of her medication goes up every few months. Ask whether she thinks that's normal, the same for everyone who uses medicines regularly, whether it would be weird to ask Jack—because he has the same type of medication. I need to hear what someone else thinks.

I don't know anyone who lives like my family does, surviving on what they produce. Perhaps other families can simply afford to pay whatever it costs.

That night, I stare at the ceiling, tracing the shadowy edge where it meets the wall. My thoughts whirr in the background, deciphering what I should do. If my parents don't sell enough produce, or something breaks and needs fixing, then maybe there won't be enough money to buy more medicine for Chloe. What will happen if we run out? I can't just wait and see. That might be too late.

The idea which began to form a few nights ago has taken shape. I reach down and slide open the drawer beneath my mattress.

I settle into my corner next to the wardrobe, resting my port-com on my knees.

The first part of my plan is simple. The information I require is straightforward too. I need to know Jack's surname, and the names of his parents. I can easily hack the school database via my messaging account.

My fingers fly across the keys.

The student database is divided into year groups. Pupils are listed alphabetically by surname. As Jack's surname is what I need to find, I'll just have to start at the top. Ten names down, I spot Jack Merril. His parents are Tom and Claudia. I continue scanning to the bottom of the list, in case there is another Jack. But he is the only one.

I leave the database, checking at every stage that I've left no clues, no markers to show that I was ever there. Then I rub my fingertips across my forehead and close my eyes. My hands hover above the keyboard. I need to concentrate. I'm going to access the system for the company which makes Chloe's medicine, using the back door JP created. The database will be huge, and it could take time to find the area I need. The area which stores customers' medical bills. But now that I know Chloe and Jack use the same medicine, at least I have something to compare. It feels like a start.

I jump from one part of the system to another, hoping that JP's back door will give me access to the right section. My legs are beginning to feel stiff. I stretch out one, then the other. I have no idea how much time has passed. I glance down at my port-watch. It's 2.30 a.m. Three hours have passed. My eyes feel dry, like they have grit in them. When I'm tired like this, I'm more likely to make mistakes.

I change tack and search for key words. Surely that will produce fewer options to explore. I'm right. I try my dad's name, which is only linked to a few areas. In one of them his name is tagged with the name of Chloe's medicine, but rather than a price, it says simply 'R8'. Frustrated, I find myself typing 'Tom Merril'. My heart thumps in my chest as his name appears, tagged with the same medicine, but rather then R8, it says Q7. I stare at the screen. What do R8 and Q7 mean? There must be a way of finding out. Something which reveals what they mean. I search, but after thirty minutes of trying, I can't find it. In desperation, I enter 'Q7' after Dad's name, to see if that produces any results.

A new interface appears. One I haven't seen before. There is a long list of two-digit codes including R8 and Q7, but no prices anywhere. Instead, at the top, are the words DATA TREATY.

A noise startles me. It's probably one of the girls turning over in their sleep. Then someone clears their throat.

I lower my screen, seconds before I hear the gentle padding of footsteps across the floor. I can't tell which direction they're heading in. A soft light glows somewhere nearby. My heart is pounding. I try not to move, but my port-com rises and falls with each breath.

The soft light drifts away. If it shines on my bed, it will be obvious that I'm not there. But whoever is awake seems to be trying hard not to disturb anyone. The bedroom door slides open, then there is silence.

I sit still for a few seconds, then as fast as I can, exit the system, leaving no trace that I was ever there.

I pad towards my bed, lift the covers and climb in, clutching my port-com to my chest, just as a pale light illuminates the doorway. I'm desperate to know who is there, but squeeze my eyes shut, as if that will somehow make me invisible. There is a rustle of fabric, then silence again. I daren't move. I will just have to sleep with my port-com on my chest. Not that I expect to sleep. Not until I work out what DATA TREATY means.

Music

'Jessica, what do you think?'

My eyes flick open. I realize with horror that I was falling asleep.

'We were talking about why our eyes see things upside down,' says Miss Fischer, pointing to the screen, where a 3D diagram of an eyeball is slowly rotating.

My head spins a little, like the eyeball.

'Something to do with the curved surface?' I say, hopefully.

'Why would that make a difference?' she asks.

My mouth feels dry, as I cast about for the answer in my sleepy brain. I sense everyone watching me.

'Because it's convex. No, wait, concave. Because our eyeballs are concave, which bends light so that it's upside down.'

'I sincerely hope they are *not* concave,' says Miss

Fischer, with an edge to her voice. 'Perhaps you could write a few lines explaining why they need to be convex, in time for our next lesson?'

I blink a few times, feeling a strangely unpleasant mix of tiredness and adrenaline.

The semi-circle seating means that there is nowhere to hide, which after two hours sleep, is exactly what I need.

I will have to try and pace myself. I wish that my extra music tuition was on Monday instead. That this afternoon was free for me to try and decipher what I saw last night.

'Jessica! Come in!' Miss Singer welcomes me warmly.

She is standing opposite two chairs in the centre of the room. Jack looks up from one of them, and smiles. It's hard to believe the same person lay pale and breathless in the corridor a few days earlier.

The room feels even bigger than usual as I cross the floor towards them. My footsteps louder.

'I've written a new piece for Jack,' I say, as I sit down.

Miss Singer beams and claps her hands together like I've just performed a brilliant trick.

My face begins to flush as I realize what I've said. 'I mean, I've written a new piece for today, I—'

'I'm sure Jack would love to play it,' Miss Singer interrupts, 'and I would love to hear it.'

Jack is already reaching for his violin case. He taps the top, and his bow and violin rise from within as if propelled by some magical force.

He holds out his hand towards me, eyes twinkling. I pass him a square of paper, crumpled like the last one. He unfolds it carefully, his eyes flicking back and forth across the lines of music. My music. He tucks the violin beneath his chin, raises the bow, and begins to play.

Even though he's never seen the piece before, the melody Jack plays is smooth and fluent. He adds lightness, and darker, louder notes in the way that I intended. Better than I'd intended.

After the final bar, he remains still for a few seconds, then lowers his bow. He turns to look at me, not Miss Singer. I stare back. What I want to say is how perfect it was. How brilliant. But I can't seem to get the words in the right order. Miss Singer comes to my rescue.

'Well,' her voice rings through the silence, 'that was beautifully played, Jack, thank you.' He nods, and sits back down, laying the violin gently across his lap. 'Jessica, a composition more intriguing than the last. The final two bars brought everything together in a way I hadn't expected.'

'Thank you.' I finally find some words.

'Before we continue with the lesson today, I have some news,' she says, her eyes sparkling. 'Twice a year, there is a competition to showcase the brightest and most promising new musical talent. Many hundreds of students enter, and a fraction of those are selected to perform live.' She pauses, looking from me to Jack. 'The performance has global reach. Our school is allowed to enter two students.' She pauses again, taking a deep breath. 'Until now, without exception, the nominated students have been from S3 or above. If you agree, I will speak to the principal to see if, for the first time ever, I can nominate students from S1.'

A spark of excitement fizzes in my chest. I glance at Jack. A small smile plays across his lips; his eyes are shining.

'Won't the other students mind?' he asks. 'The ones in the older years?'

'Our policy has been to nominate from older year groups, but the submission brief states "most promising musical talent". This year, Jack and Jessica, that is you.'

'Has anyone from our school been chosen to perform live?' I ask, my heart thumping.

'No,' Miss Singer says. 'But those who do, secure many options for future appearances and potentially a musical career. They also receive free instruments and equipment,' she adds, being careful not to look at my violin and case as she says this.

'So—how do we enter?' I ask.

'Simple. We choose a piece to play and submit a recording.'

'But,' I frown. 'Jack is better than me. Shouldn't you enter Jack and someone from another year group?'

'You are a gifted musician,' Miss Singer says. 'What makes you even more exceptional is your ability to create original scores. To write fantastic music that showcases what you and Jack can do. I would like you to play, Jessica, and I would also like you to write the music.'

I begin to understand what Miss Singer is asking. She wants me to compose a duet.

I nod slowly. My mind starting to whirr. 'That would be—I mean, that sounds—yes please. Thank you.'

I feel my cheeks glow. Miss Singer and Jack are both smiling.

'Well, let's hope that the principal agrees. In the meantime, Jessica, can I listen to you play?'

As Jack leans back in his chair, I glimpse the top of his violin case. I hadn't noticed before but on the top, in silvery script, are the letters JM. Jack Merril.

Truth

I barely remember getting into bed last night. For the first time ever, I was asleep before Ana. JP was going to send a new challenge, but I'll have to wait until later to see what it is. I try to concentrate during morning lessons, but tiredness makes it harder to block out the questions swirling round my head. DATA TREATY, Charlie Scott, Mae's school. I'm used to finding patterns, solutions, without even trying. But these fragments take me nowhere, the pieces of the puzzle are too incomplete to see any pattern or picture.

Just before lunch, my port-watch buzzes. As I leave the classroom, I glance down to see a message from Mae.

Meet during Kin Space. Under the oak.

She is sitting in the same place as before. She watches as I walk across the grass towards her. This time she isn't waving.

'Hey,' she says.

'Hey,' I reply, joining her on the damp grass. I want to fix things.

I wait for her to speak.

She is watching me. She doesn't look cross, but she doesn't say anything either. Instead she picks at a blade of grass. It occurs to me that she might be feeling bad too. That for the first time since I met her, she isn't sure what to say.

'Does your mum–' I pause and look around to check that no one is nearby, even though no one else ever comes this far across the field apart from when we are doing sport. 'Does your mum still have her own school?'

My words sound strange. The idea so unlikely that as soon as I've asked the question, I begin to doubt whether that's what Mae said the first time.

'She does.' Mae hesitates. 'Jess, I'm sorry about the way I spoke to you. I was wrong. You were right. I should have given you a chance. I've never talked to anyone about home before–apart from people who already know about it.' Mae seems to be choosing her words carefully. 'And I want you to know about it too.'

I smile.

'Mum's been running her school for nine years. Since I was old enough to start live-learning. She didn't want me learning from a screen.' She pauses. 'Even if the lessons were "live". At first there was just me and her, in the shed at the bottom of the garden. Then another kid joined. Mum tried to keep it quiet, but word seemed to spread. More kids arrived. We ran out of space, and when someone offered us an old barn, we moved the school there. Mum didn't actually call it a school. She called it *The Barn*, and we were the *Barn Kids*. When I left, she had about forty. Dad was starting to get seriously worried that she might be arrested, but Mum said people wouldn't send their kids if they didn't feel the same way about live-learning. And anyway, they'd get themselves into trouble too.'

I gasp. 'Forty kids, all under the age of fourteen?'

Mae nods.

Now I try to choose my words carefully, too. 'After the antibiotics stopped working, I thought they made all kinds of laws to protect us.'

'They did,' says Mae. 'But that was twenty years ago, during the Scarlet Fever epidemic. It's safe to meet people now. But live-learning seems better—especially with holograms. You can sit with your class, without having to leave home. It's easier.'

'So,' I try to get my thoughts in order, 'why not change the law anyway and give people a choice? Why is it still illegal?'

'Think about it,' says Mae. 'There's a lot of money to be made from keeping people in one place, with only their screens. Think of all the shopping for a start. Why change things if most people are happy? Give them more incentives like new hologram sets, or VR kits instead. Mum says that money makes the world go round. Not truth. The ones making all the money are smart. They're very generous to the people who made the laws, so they won't rush to change them. She says people are more likely to believe lots of half-truths, if that fits what they want to believe, than the actual truth itself. She–'

Mae's eyes dart upwards to something behind me.

I spin round. Students are spilling onto the field, clutching hockey sticks and footballs.

'Oh no!' I jump to my feet. 'We're *so* late for hockey.'

Before I can run back towards the changing rooms, Mae grabs my arm.

'Now that you know my secret, Jess, maybe you should tell me yours.' When I look at her, confused, she adds, 'What is it you do on your port-com every night?' The corners of her mouth lift in a small smile, but there is an intensity to the way she's looking at me, which makes it clear she won't be happy with anything less than the whole truth.

Friend

As the glow from the solar magnifier fades, the light above my desk clicks on. It must be dusk. I've been in the quiet study zone for several hours. Like Finn, I suddenly have a lot of homework. I also need to work on my new composition, and JP has sent me a challenge. I checked last night. But as I sat by the wardrobe, in the blueish glow of my port-com screen, I couldn't stop wondering whether Mae was awake too, and if Mae was awake, who else might be watching. I didn't want to linger. There was no time to start. No time to hack back into the pharma system, either.

I rest my chin on my hand as Mae's question echoes round my head. *What is it you do?* Mae shared her secret with me. If I tell her nothing about mine, then how can we be proper friends? But my secret feels bigger. The laws I've broken more serious.

I tap the side of my desk. The screen and keyboard vanish inside.

I need a change of scene, so I wander slowly over to the music room.

Halfway there, I hear the sound of footsteps behind me.

A quiet voice says, 'Jess.'

I spin round. Jack is walking down the corridor towards me.

'I saw you in the study room,' he says. Which is funny because I didn't see him. 'I just wanted to say thank you.'

'What for?'

'For helping me the other day when I was—unwell. I would have felt a lot worse if you hadn't acted so quickly.'

'Oh, that's OK, I'm used to it.'

He tilts his head, confused.

'I mean, I've seen one of those masks before. I knew what to do.'

'Well, thanks anyway.' He hesitates for a second. 'Would you like to work on the new piece together—before our next Friday session with Miss Singer?'

I nod.

'How about Thursday?'

'Perfect,' I say.

He smiles, then heads back down the corridor, the way he came.

Perhaps I should have told him about Chloe, but my life from home—my secrets, seem to be scattering like leaves in the wind. I want to feel in control of them again, first.

I peer through the small window in the door of the music room. No one's there. But then, I didn't really expect there to be.

I wander over to the window. Beneath is a small table looking onto the drive, beyond that a cluster of oak trees, like at the bottom of the meadow. I watch their dark outlines sway in the breeze, silhouetted by dusk. Disjointed melodies sway back and forth in my head too. Jack mentioned the new piece, but I haven't written anything yet. The harder I concentrate, the more elusive the melody seems to be. Instead, I end up thinking about Jack smiling at me before he walked away.

There is a tapping sound. I look around the room as the door slides open and Mae bursts in.

'This was my last resort! I've been looking everywhere for you. You know you've missed dinner, right?'

I glance towards the window. The oak silhouettes have melted into black night sky.

'I saved you something.' She holds up a banana and two bread rolls.

'You're amazing,' I smile, gathering up my paper and pencil. 'Thank you. I didn't notice the time.' I rub my eyes, which feel dry and prickly, as if they've just heard how late it is too.

'Come on, we should hurry,' she adds. 'We'll be in trouble if anyone finds us here. It's almost time for FOG.'

'Seriously? It's *that* late?' I get to my feet and walk quickly to the door, which Mae is holding open with her foot.

'Mae—wait a second.' I move her foot so that the door slides shut again. She looks at me as if I've really lost the plot. But I haven't. I've made a decision. 'On my port-com,' I say softly, 'at night—I'm hacking. I never do anything bad, it's just for fun, but I don't think that's how most people view cybercrime. Anyway, now you know. Perhaps best to keep it to yourself, though, because the government definitely *does* have laws about that.'

Mae swallows, but holds my gaze, nodding slowly. 'OK. I can definitely keep that to myself.'

She passes me the banana and the bread rolls. Suddenly, though, I don't feel so much like eating.

Empty

'It's gone!' cries a voice from the other side of the dormitory.

I glance up but carry on getting ready. Lessons start in five minutes.

Nyla fumbles to remove her port-watch then throws it on the bed. 'All my stuff!' She whimpers, eyes wide with panic.

'What happened?' Violet asks, breaking the strange silence which has descended on the dormitory.

'My ROOM. It's empty. Everything's gone! All my ROOMmates will leave,' she replies, her voice shaking.

A chorus of gasps ripples across the room.

'Have you rebooted?' asks Violet. 'Check the filter isn't set to "redecorate", oh, and make sure you haven't switched on "total revamp".'

Nyla shakes her head. 'I've done everything. It's

empty. Every single room. It's like—it's like I've been deleted.' She runs her fingers through her spiky hair.

There are more murmurs but no one says anything audible.

Violet crosses over to Nyla's bed, which is opposite hers, and sits on the edge. 'Shall I have a look?' She points to the watch.

Nyla nods, tears glistening in her eyes.

Everyone starts peering at their wrists, talking softly to the screens, making sure nothing unusual has happened. I look down at my own and see that there is a message from Chloe.

I've created an automatic cypher, so that I can decode her messages when they arrive, rather than several hours later.

Cannot get in to live-learning. Not since Thursday. Mum and Dad being weird about it. Might go and see the goats. Miss you. Kit says miaow x Chloe

I read the message again, and a creeping sense of unease shivers down my spine. Perhaps it's because everyone in the dorm seems on edge this morning, or maybe it's because in the eight years I had live-learning, there was never a single day when it didn't work.

I pull on my socks and trainers and head for the door, past Violet and Nyla, huddled on the bed, still trying to work out where Nyla's ROOM has gone.

As I hurry to language studies my watch buzzes again. It's a message from Mum.

Darling, in case you decide to port-com, we won't be at home tomorrow. We're taking some produce to a new client.

This is big news. They hardly ever use the transport—Mum and Dad coordinate their honey and cheese deliveries weeks in advance.

Nothing to worry about. We thought it would be fun.

If Mum and Dad are suddenly taking on new clients, it can only mean one thing. They are running out of credits.

Skill

The next few days rush past in a haze of schoolwork. There is no time to port-com home. Mum needn't have worried. I struggle to keep up with the homework we receive for almost every lesson, then Mr Hoff announces there will be an assessment on the programming techniques we've learnt over the last two weeks. He says it's not a test, but I'm sure it is. After the last 'not-a-test', two students moved out of our group, and two new ones joined. The new ones put their hands up first, every time Mr Hoff asks a question.

On Thursday afternoon, I head straight to the music room after lessons. Jack is already there, practising scales by the window. As the door slides open, he lifts his bow.

'Sorry I'm late,' I say. 'I forgot my violin. I mean, I came straight from geography and then had to go back up to my dorm to get it.' I realize that I'm rambling.

'No worries, I've only been here a few minutes,' he smiles.

I put my violin case on the floor. It looks shabbier than usual next to Jack's silvery hard-shelled carrier.

'I haven't written anything down yet. I thought I could play you some melodies on the piano, then we can see what's working.'

'Good idea.'

'I've only ever composed on my own before.'

Jack rests his violin on the chair and walks to the piano with me. His footsteps are light. He moves quietly, a bit like the tiger cubs which have been prowling round the dormitory.

'I don't know how you come up with so many ideas. It takes me ages. I've only done it a few times. Outside lessons, anyway.'

'I just like patterns, I guess. I like programming too.'

He nods. 'I think playing is my skill.'

I fetch some manuscript paper from my violin case and scribble down the melodies as I play, stopping every few bars to make changes or add new sections which Jack has suggested. After about an hour, my pages look as if someone has attacked them with a pencil.

'Why don't you use a screen?' he asks. 'It would be much easier to make changes and share.'

I shrug. 'I like writing it down. It feels more real,' I say. I glance at my port-watch. It's almost time for dinner. 'I should probably copy it out again before we play any more, though. I guess it is getting a *bit* hard to see what I've written.'

'It sounds really great so far, Jess. I think we might be in with a chance.'

A warm feeling fizzes in my stomach.

'Thank you. Let's hope Miss Singer likes it too.'

I zip up my case. Jack's violin glides silently into the silver carrier.

'See you tomorrow,' he says, pushing his dark hair away from his eyes.

'Tomorrow,' I say, and give a small wave as he heads to the door.

After he's gone, I feel a rush of disappointment when I realize that I've missed Kin Space again.

But there's a message from Chloe on my port-watch.

Hey Jessyloo. Did Mum tell you? We didn't go anywhere on Tuesday after all. Dad thought he'd charged the transport, but he hadn't. Then they realized that it had been plugged in all night, but the charger wasn't working. I still can't get into live-learning. Mum and Dad stop talking every time I walk into the room. Kit doesn't understand what's going on. Neither do I. I'm in bed too. Poorly again. Bad yesterday and today. Miss you. Chlo x

The sense of uneasiness swirls in my chest again. I re-read the message. Mum and Dad can't charge the transport, Chloe can't get into live-learning. I don't understand what's going on either. Perhaps it's just coincidence. I try to stay calm. I want to reassure Chloe, but I also want someone to reassure me. What might Mum and Dad be hiding from her?

Chloe's poorly again too. I know that when she has episodes close together, it's harder for Mum and Dad to control her symptoms. The chance of needing hospital treatment is much higher. And we can't afford hospital treatment.

'Hey Chlo,' I say to my port-watch. *'Maybe there's been a power outage somewhere and that's why they can't charge the transport. Don't worry about live-learning. A week isn't much to miss for a super-smart student like you. Maybe it's time you gave the other kids a chance anyway. In case it makes you feel better, midnight feasts have been cancelled here. Biscuit shortage. I might need you and Kit to come and rescue me, or at the very least deliver some biscuits. Give her a tickle behind the ears from me. Jessylooooooo x.'*

Straight afterwards, I send a message to Mum and Dad, asking them to port-com tomorrow.

I know that when I see them, I'll feel much better.

Drones

When I get back to the dorm, I realize something has happened. As the door slides open, whoops of excitement ring along the corridor.

Several girls are huddled round Nyla's bed, and a few others are perched on Violet's, port-watches raised.

Eve says, 'Look at this one! It has luminescent sleeves.'

'Choose the cinema setting. Select your seat fabric first, then it's easier to match the other elements,' adds Ana.

I walk slowly over to my bed, trying to work out what's going on. I guess Nyla's ROOM is fixed, at least.

Mae is waiting for me, her chin resting on her hand.

'Gala Night,' she mouths. 'Everyone has gone nuts. Who knew that's all it would take?' She sits up, making space on the bed for me.

'What's Gala Night?' I ask, frowning.

'On Saturday evening we'll have a special meal, then an *immersive cinema experience* in the main hall. 4D, sound and movement—the works. Have you not read your school alerts?'

'Not in the last hour,' I say.

'Well, now you've got to make up for lost time. They're ordering outfits and creating cinema ROOMS for their ROOMmates.' Mae rolls her eyes towards the others.

'That is very—cool,' I say, trying to sound excited, even though my mind is on Chloe's message.

Mae assumes I'm being sarcastic.

'I know. It does seem a bit crazy,' she agrees. 'I think it might actually be fun, though. You don't have to dress up if you don't want to.'

After dinner, everyone carries on manically planning and ordering. I wanted something fun to happen. Now that it is, I am the one who wants to be alone with my screen.

I'm desperate to go back into the pharma database. To investigate DATA TREATY. If Mum and Dad have run out of credits, things are worse than I feared. But a few minutes after the housemaster has checked for

FOG, everyone sits up in bed again, whispering to their port-watches.

I won't have a chance tonight.

On Friday morning, I am woken by a swarm of drones arriving with new outfits and accessories.

I check my port-watch. There is no message from Mum or Dad. No message from Chloe either. I'm sure they will be in touch later. They're probably busy outside. Maybe one of the goats has escaped.

In the programming assessment I come joint-first. With Violet. I was trying to come second.

'Well done,' she says, brushing past me on her way to the door.

'Thank you.'

'For being lucky, I mean. Luck doesn't last though,' she snaps.

I didn't want to come first, but I feel frustrated that Violet expects to. That she believes only bad luck can prevent it.

When lessons finish, I'm about to head to the quiet study zone, when I remember my session with Miss Singer. I can't believe I almost forgot. As I approach the music room, I feel a flutter in my stomach. I must be nervous about sharing what Jack and I have worked on.

'Would you like the good news first?' Miss Singer asks, clutching her port-screen so tightly that I wonder whether it might snap.

Jack pushes his hair from his eyes. His calm stillness the exact opposite.

'The principal has agreed that you will be our nominees for this year's competition, and I've received a message,' she says, holding her screen in the air, 'confirming that you've been invited to submit a complete song or musical piece.'

I gasp.

Jack is nodding his head and smiling. 'When do we have to submit the full piece?'

'Ah.' Miss Singer's smile falters slightly. 'We need to submit within two weeks.'

Jack makes a low whistling sound.

'Yes, it doesn't leave us much time. I wondered whether you might be willing to give up a few evenings to prepare?'

'Count me in,' Jack says quickly. 'Jess?' He looks over.

'Definitely,' I reply.

'Jessica, have you had any time to think about a piece, along the lines of what we discussed? The majority of entrants will be playing their own versions of pre-existing songs.' She pauses. 'So it's fine if you two would like to do the same. I realize this is a lot of extra work for the start of your first school year.' Her eyes flick from me to Jack.

'We've already been working on something. It's not finished, but–'

'It's brilliant,' Jack says, his eyes shining.

The flutter in my stomach spreads upwards to my chest.

Miss Singer shakes her head, as if not quite believing what she's heard.

'Well, you've certainly hit the ground running,' she smiles. 'Can you play me what you have so far?'

I tap the music stand and the screen unfurls.

'Version four,' I say clearly.

Jack stares at me, a smile twitching the corners of his mouth.

'You digitized it?'

I nod. 'Not because it's better. There were just too many corrections.'

'Shall we begin?' Miss Singer asks.

Jack lifts his bow. As I rest my violin on my shoulder, everything in the room seems sharper, clearer. I've felt this way before, but only when I'm hacking.

'I thought we were being invaded by giant wasps this morning,' says Mae, as we head through the common room back to the dorm.

'I'm surprised there were no collisions,' I reply. 'Between the drones, or between everyone rushing to collect their parcels.'

Mae laughs.

The atmosphere in the dormitory is calmer tonight. All the packages have been opened and examined. After FOG, everyone stays in bed, exhausted by endless fabric decisions.

Even so, I wait extra-long, until I'm sure they are all asleep. As sure as I can be.

As I sit silently on the floor next to the wardrobe, I realize I'm not the same Jess who sat here last week. The routines I took for granted, the things in my life which felt certain, fixed, are all changing.

I send a quick message to JP. I say that the challenge is good. That I'm enjoying it, and not to worry, I'll crack it soon. It's a basic CTF. I need to Capture the Flag–the bad piece of code–which JP has hidden in a file. Like looking for the worm in an apple. I haven't started.

Instead I begin the routine to connect to the pharma database. But rather than the access page, a No Entry sign flashes in the centre of my screen.

An icy chill trickles down my spine. Someone knows I was in the system.

I must have left a trace.

I knew I was tired. That I should have stopped sooner. I was distracted, too. Desperately, I try to replay every step in my head, but I cannot find an answer. What did I do?

As I walk back over to my bed, my legs feel unsteady. I slide my port-com gently into the drawer. Then lie down, my face buried in the pillow. Tonight, I feel glad that Mae knows my secret. Glad that she is my friend.

Weird

On Saturday morning there are still no messages from home. I take my port-com to the common room during Kin Space. I thought it would be empty, but everyone wants to share their Gala Night purchases. Eve has put on her new outfit. Others simply hold things up to show. There are no spare tables, so I sit on the floor, my port-com on my lap. It feels strangely similar to the space I occupy every night, next to the wardrobe. I stay for half an hour, but the screen remains blank. I think about messaging Finn instead, but I don't know what to tell him about Mum and Dad.

After hockey, I get changed slowly. I'm in no hurry to go back to the dormitory.

'Penny for your thoughts?' Mae thumps down on the bench next to me.

'Who says *penny for your thoughts* any more?'

'I do.'

'Have you ever seen a penny?'

'I have, actually. When everyone switched to digital money, my mum kept some notes and coins. She uses them in class.'

I smile. Then my smile fades when I remember what I was thinking about before Mae arrived.

'So?' she says.

'Oh, I just haven't heard from my parents much, and a few weird things have been happening.'

'Weird?'

'Chloe can't get onto live-learning, Mum and Dad can't charge the transport.' As I say it out loud, I realize how silly it sounds.

'Power cut?' suggests Mae.

I nod. 'That's what I thought. That's what I told Chloe, anyway.'

'Well, I'm going to the dorm so that I can spend the next two hours making myself look incredible. Care to join me?'

I push myself to my feet. 'Is it OK if I only spend two minutes?'

'Totally,' says Mae. 'You're a natural beauty.'

I don't mention Chloe being ill. Not because it's secret. I don't want it to feel so real.

*

I change into a dress which Mum made for me out of dark green velvet. It looks 'old style', but that's what I love about it.

I look across to Mae's bed, to see what she's wearing. She's still in her leggings and hoodie, but she beckons me over.

I walk past Nyla who is struggling into a stretchy jumpsuit, spangled with gold flecks. Eve is standing nearby, perhaps ready to help if the stretchy material starts winning.

'I thought you weren't interested in getting dressed up,' Mae says accusingly. 'You look amazing. Where did you get that dress?'

'My mum made it.'

Eve glances across. She looks at the dress, but not at me.

'I'm not sure I believe you. Well now I wish I'd spent a few more hours choosing mine. I'm not sure whether I should give you this, either.'

'What?' I ask, sitting on the corner of her bed.

'Close your eyes and put out your hand.'

I do as instructed. Mae places something cold and slightly spiky in my hand.

I open my eyes and gasp. In my palm rests a bee, crafted from hundreds of tiny crystals, on a delicate frame of silver-coloured metal.

'It's a clip,' says Mae, taking the bee from my hand and sliding it into the hair above my right ear. 'Keep still.'

She holds up her wrist and scans me with her port-watch. Then she takes off the watch so that I can have a proper look.

The clip nestles within my chestnut-coloured hair, glinting silver and gold. It turns my velvety outfit into something glamorous. I love it.

'Can I wear it tonight?'

'It's yours,' says Mae. 'It's nowhere near as expensive as it looks, but I overheard you talking to your mum and dad about beehives and honey harvests, so, well, now you have a bee of your own.'

I hug Mae. 'Thank you. Chloe will want one too.'

'I think Jack might like it as well,' whispers Mae.

I feel my cheeks burn.

'I really have to start getting ready. Especially now that you look like that.' She picks up two dresses and holds them next to each other.

'The red one,' I say, then wander back to my bed, a warm feeling glowing in my chest.

There's still half an hour or so until the Gala begins. The perfect chance to read for a bit. I lift the lid of my trunk. The hinges make a low creaking noise, which I'm fairly sure didn't happen before.

I choose a book with a swirling sea design on the front. Dad read it to me and Chloe a few years ago. He would sit on the floor next to the bed and read a little bit each night. Chloe and I would squash up together on her bunk, trying not to make a noise so that Dad might forget we were there, and keep on reading to the next chapter. I place it on the pillow. Then I reach for Dad's thin grey coding book. I hold it close to my face and breathe in the papery smell. I thumb through the pages. Pages I have looked at hundreds of times. I'm about to place it back in the trunk when something on the title page catches my eye. I've seen it before, of course. I've just never taken any notice of it. It didn't mean anything then. It does mean something now, though. Written in pale blue ink, at the top of the page, nearest the spine, are the letters *CS*.

Spy

The next evening, the dining hall is half empty. I sit alone at the table. Everyone has chosen to go to bed early rather than eat. The immersive film was good—an undersea adventure—but unlike the others, I didn't stay up until the early hours, curating my ROOM space afterwards. I needed a clear head today to scale the mountain of homework growing silently within my port-com. I check my port-watch for messages. For the twentieth time. There are none. I realize it's been eleven days since I saw my family sitting on the bench in the garden. Hot tears sting the corners of my eyes. I place my tray on the neat-bot and get up to leave.

When I reach the common room, I feel a tap on my shoulder.

I wipe my eyes before turning round.

'What is it? What's the matter?' It's Mae. Her eyes dart around my face, trying to work out what's happened. 'Let's sit down for a bit.' She points to a sofa by the window.

I perch on the edge, one foot tucked beneath me, and take a few slow breaths to calm myself down. I don't want to sound hysterical.

'It's about my mum and dad,' I say.

Mae nods encouragingly. As I begin to tell her—again—what's been going on, it doesn't sound silly any more.

'I can't get in touch with them. They haven't answered my port-messages for days. Now Chloe isn't answering hers, either. The transport wouldn't charge, live-learning has disconnected. It's like they've disappeared and I need to know how Chloe is. She's been really poorly again.' I hear the quiver in my voice.

Mae hears it too. She nods slowly, thoughtfully. My mouth feels dry. The sense of unease is turning into something else. Fear.

'Maybe they didn't see the messages. Perhaps they've just been really busy.'

I shake my head, not trusting myself to speak straight away. 'Not for this long.'

'But you're still getting messages from Chloe?'

'Well, I was. But I messaged her yesterday, and she hasn't replied. It's like–' I hesitate. 'It's like my family has vanished.' Tears pool at the bottom of my eyes again. This time I can't stop them from spilling down my cheeks.

'Jess, there must be a good explanation.'

I want to feel reassured by Mae's words. But there is a heavy sensation in my chest. I've been through every good explanation I can think of. Connections hardly ever fail, and if they do, then it never takes more than a few hours before they're fixed. Otherwise we couldn't live the way we do. Which can only mean one thing. Something is seriously wrong.

I glance at Mae. Her chin is propped on the heel of her hand. She's gazing straight ahead, but not as if she's thinking about what I said. Her gaze is more intense. She's looking at something. I turn round. Dangling over the side of the opposite armchair, is a pair of feet. I recognize the trainers. Violet is sitting in the chair, and she must have heard everything.

'I'm really tired,' says Mae, yawning loudly.

'So am I,' I sniff. I realize what Mae is doing, but I also wonder when we will be able to talk again; wonder what I should do now. Maybe I should speak to a teacher. But they would suggest doing exactly what I have been doing. Send a message and wait.

I'm about to follow Mae to the door, when a voice says, 'I think you're right to worry.'

I look over to the chair where Violet's feet were dangling. Her feet have disappeared, replaced by her head, as she leans round the side of the chair.

'I said, I think you're right to worry.'

The voice is quiet. Matter of fact.

Mae freezes, halfway between the sofa and the door, staring, mouth slightly open, at the back of the chair containing Violet.

'Do you want to know why?'

I feel myself nod.

'Of course she does!' says Mae, striding back across the common room. As Violet comes into view, she stops, her hands on her hips.

'I was talking to Jess,' Violet says defiantly.

'Well, I was talking to Jess too. We were having a *private* conversation.'

'Oh,' says Violet. 'Well I didn't want to listen to your *private* conversation, but I didn't have any choice, did I? If you don't want my help, that's fine. I'd rather go and brush my teeth anyway.'

'No. Please,' I say, 'Mae didn't mean to be rude.' I sense Mae scowling at me.

'Yes, she did,' says Violet, 'but if *you* want my help then I'll stay.'

'I do.'

Mae thumps down on the sofa next to me but keeps quiet.

Violet looks from Mae to me, where her eyes linger.

'Is it correct that your parents cannot access live-learning, or transport-charging credits, and have not been able to connect to their port-watches or screens either?'

'Well,' I say slowly, piecing together what Violet has absorbed so quickly. 'Yes, I think that sounds right.'

'And were credits unavailable for other purchases too?'

'I don't know,' I frown, wondering how I could tell whether my parents have been able to pay for anything recently. 'We don't have a lot of credits anyway.'

'What about your parents' emergency trip?' Mae says, an edge of excitement to her voice.

'They were going to meet a new client. To sell extra produce,' I confirm. If Violet thinks this sounds weird, she doesn't let it show. 'It did seem quite sudden.'

'Like they suddenly needed credits?' adds Mae triumphantly.

'I suppose that's possible.'

'Well, Violet,' Mae says, 'what does it all mean? You said you were going to help. So far you've just told us what we already know.'

I'm worried that if Mae carries on, Violet will leave. Her face is in the shadow of the armchair, but her blue eyes sparkle as they flit round my face. Then it dawns on me. She already knows the answer. She's deciding whether to tell me.

'The housemaster will be here any second for FOG,' says Mae, 'and we're not even ready for bed.'

'Can you keep a secret?' Violet asks.

Mae snorts, but Violet ignores her.

'Yes. I'm good at keeping secrets,' I answer.

'Because what I'm going to tell you could get me in trouble. It could get my family in trouble. Although I'm less worried about that.'

I feel my heart thumping faster in my chest.

'I know what has happened to your parents.' She hesitates, then says, 'They've been deleted.'

'That doesn't actually happen. Not for real,' says Mae.

I look from Mae to Violet. I've never heard of being *deleted*.

'It's a fairy tale,' Mae adds angrily, 'to make sure people behave. Like the fairy tale which says we still have to stay at home.'

I know Mae is trying to help, but I wish she would let Violet speak.

'But–what does it mean?' I ask.

'It means that you don't exist any more,' says Mae. 'Not for real. You don't exist digitally.'

I feel my insides turn to ice.

'Everything about you is erased. You can't buy things, connect to anyone, search for anything. You might as well not exist for real either. But, like I said, it's a fairy tale.'

'No, it's not,' says Violet quietly.

'How do you know?' Mae stares at Violet. 'Jess is worried about her parents. Spreading rubbish like this has made her feel ten times worse. It's how stupid rumours become "facts".'

Mae gets to her feet again. I think she expects me to join her, but I'm watching Violet. She seems calm. Confident.

'It's not a fairy tale,' she repeats, in the same quiet voice. 'I know it's not a fairy tale, because my dad invented it.'

There is a gentle swish as the door to the common room slides open. I turn to see the housemaster stop abruptly near the entrance. She wasn't expecting to see anyone here. She converts surprise to mild outrage by folding her arms across her chest.

'I'm not going to ask what you're doing, but FOG applies to all students. Upstairs now, please. I will be checking the dormitory in five minutes, and I expect everyone in bed, lights out. OK?'

'Yes, Mrs Drew,' we agree, hurrying towards the door.

Exactly five minutes later, a pale rectangle of light illuminates the corner of the dormitory, and a silhouette of the housemaster appears. After a minute, the silhouette retreats. The rectangle of light disappears and the dormitory melts back into shades of grey.

As I stare at the ceiling, it feels as if sleep will be impossible tonight. I'm sure Mae and Violet must be lying awake, too.

The question which echoes round and round my head is why? Why would anyone want to 'delete' my parents? It makes no sense at all.

Gone

I become aware of someone shaking me gently by the shoulder.

'You're going to miss breakfast.'

I open my eyes. Mae is crouched next to my bed. There are dusky shadows beneath her eyes.

As I sit up, fragments of last night's conversation swirl round my head.

'Come on!' she urges.

In the dining hall, I feel as if everybody knows what we talked about, even though no one pays me any attention as I place fruit and toast on my tray.

I don't feel like eating. There is an uncomfortable knot in my stomach.

Violet is sitting in the same chair as usual. She doesn't look up when I sit down. Only Mae is buzzing with a nervous kind of energy. The yoghurt jar slides from her plate as she leans towards the neat-bot, clattering to the table, but not breaking. I'm almost relieved she has to leave early to finish some homework.

Violet places her tray on the neat-bot too. Before she stands up, I try to catch her eye.

'Violet.'

She looks over. For a split second her expression changes—reflecting the same energy Mae's did.

'Will you be outside at break time?' I ask.

'Not at break time.'

'At lunch time, maybe?' I realize my voice is slightly too high. There is a pleading edge to it.

'I can meet you by the tree, if you like,' she says.

'OK.' I nod. The knot in my stomach loosens a little.

The morning passes in slow motion. Halfway through plant science my port-watch vibrates. It should be in sleep mode, but I don't want to miss a message from Mum or Dad. I glance down at my wrist. It's from Finn. It occurs to me that he might have some news. The teacher is still talking. I need to at least look as if I'm listening. I can't risk having my port-watch confiscated.

A hologram of a tulip hovers in the centre of the room, the petals and outer layers gently peeling away to reveal a magnified interior, before reforming to repeat the display. We are supposed to label it. Using my finger, I trace a line to the words *style* and *stigma.* As I begin the next line, I let my hand linger mid-air, and read the message.

Send news! And scrambled egg sandwiches! Port-com later? F x

My shoulders sag a little. Finn doesn't have news, he wants it—which means he can't have heard from Chloe either. A shadow falls across my desk. Miss Ali is standing directly in front of me. I pretend not to have noticed and continue tracing, trying to focus on what I'm doing.

When the low bell sounds for lunch, I'm still only halfway through and my labels are a mess. There isn't time to correct them.

I head straight to the dining room. There's no queue yet. I don't feel hungry, but I know I should eat something. I grab some fruit and a sandwich. I'm about to message Mae, to say that I will meet her later, when she slides into the seat next to me.

'Will you wait? I'll be quick,' she says, taking an extra-large spoonful of rice.

I'd hoped to meet Violet on my own. I'm worried that Mae will lose her temper again and Violet will actually leave this time. There's no way I can go without her now, though.

Eve and Nyla sit down a few seats away.

'Mae,' I say quietly, 'Violet said she'd meet me—meet us—by the tree. I really want to hear what she has to say.'

Mae nods. 'I'll be on my best behaviour, if that's what you mean,' she adds through a mouthful of food.

I didn't spot Violet in the dining hall, but when we walk out into the yard, she is beneath the tree already. As we get closer, I see that she's brought a waterproof square to sit on. She watches us approach, unsmiling.

'Hi. I don't have long,' she says briskly.

'That's OK,' I say. 'So—' The questions I'm so desperate to ask seem to tumble towards my mouth all at once.

'You want to know what's happening?' Violet asks.

Mae shifts on the grass next to me, but she stays quiet.

'Yes,' I nod. 'Are my parents—is my family going to be OK?'

'Web connections don't fail by accident. The systems are too good. When our parents were our age, connections used to fail all the time. Bad systems, bad security, bad infrastructure.'

Violet sounds like a live-learning teacher addressing a class.

'There's no reason why your mother's port-watch shouldn't work. But assuming that some kind of anomalous and extremely rare hardware failure has occurred, the chances of that same failure affecting your father's port-watch is almost zero. In addition, live-learning has deactivated and they cannot access their credits.' She pauses, as if to check that I am keeping up.

I nod. My heart is thumping in my chest. She has analysed my conversation with Mae so precisely.

'My father works for Global Connections, which controls ninety per cent of all portal sites. He is head of their security department.'

Violet pauses again, her blue eyes shining. Her chin lifts slightly as she talks about her dad, there is a note of something different in her voice, too. As if she's tasted something unpleasant.

'He doesn't discuss what he does. But I hear him in meetings sometimes, and when he speaks to Mum. When they think I'm not listening.' From the way Violet says this, I get the feeling they often assume she's not listening.

'He says that the only way to stop cybercrime is quickly. That every second counts.'

Mae looks at her port-watch. I don't care what time it is. I won't let Violet stop until I know everything that she does.

'Because Global Connections is international, ubiquitous, normal laws can't apply. They are too slow. If cybercrime is detected it must be shut down immediately, to limit damage and prevent repeat offences.

Your cyber accounts and all online presence will be deactivated. You will be deleted.'

'Woah,' says Mae. 'How can *that* be legal?'

'Like I said, normal laws can't apply,' Violet replies sharply.

'What do you have to do?' I ask slowly. 'I mean, to commit cybercrime?'

'Stealing credits, faking information,' she hesitates, 'and hacking.'

Mae glances my way for a fraction of a second. But Violet misses nothing.

The palms of my hands feel damp. I need to stay calm. I need a clear head.

But my mind is racing. Everything Violet says is clear. Precise. It makes sense. What doesn't make sense is how this could have happened to my family. I'm the hacker, but my port-com is set up with a private network of its own. It's almost impossible to discover my true identity. And Mum and Dad barely use their screens. There's simply no way they could be cybercriminals.

Now Violet checks her port-watch.

'If you tell anyone what I've told you about my father, I will deny it. I will also make sure that Mae's family is deleted,' Violet adds, in the same matter-of-fact way she has said everything else.

Mae gasps.

'Why would I tell anyone else?' I ask.

Violet shrugs, as if what other people do is a mystery to her. She gets to her feet and shakes the waterproof square. 'I ordered it as soon as we agreed to meet here.' When I look blank she adds, 'Rapid drone service.'

'Violet.' I take a deep breath in and out. 'I know you said that the security system is never wrong, but if my parents have been deleted, it must be some kind of mistake. They would never do any of the things you mentioned.'

'I'm sorry,' says Violet. 'I thought you would say that. But the system is never wrong.'

I feel a tight sensation across my chest.

'Then—how can I help them?'

'There's nothing you can do.'

Without warning, the tightness whirls into a spark of anger.

'Then why did you make me come over here to talk about it?'

'I didn't. You asked to meet me.'

'Well why tell me about it at all!' I throw my hands in the air. I realize I'm beginning to sound like Mae.

'Perhaps I shouldn't have,' she says. 'I just thought you'd want to know. I would want to know.' Her face is even more pale than usual.

Violet rolls up her mat, then sets off towards the school building.

I want to call after her, to make her stay, to make her help me. But I know it won't do any good. She said there's nothing I can do. Even if there was, I doubt she'd help me now. Mae managed to hold her temper, but I didn't. With each step Violet takes, I feel my anger ebbing away, replaced with a heavy feeling, spreading from somewhere deep inside me.

How could this possibly be happening? I want to speak to Mum, or to Dad. To tell them what Violet told me. I want to see them, to see Chloe. To know what's happened to them. Whether this is real.

'Jess?' Mae's voice breaks my train of thought. 'We have to go. Are you OK?'

I nod, although it's obvious that I'm not. Even Mae doesn't know what to say.

'Let's just make it through this afternoon's lessons, then I'll meet you straight afterwards.'

'I have extra music,' I say, automatically. Realizing that I haven't even told Mae about the competition yet.

'Well after that, then. Come on.'

Alone

'Shall we try that one more time?'

Miss Singer's eyes linger on me as I lower my bow. I've messed up the same bar four times.

I know this piece by heart, but every time I begin to play, Violet's words echo round my head. *There's nothing you can do.*

I take a deep breath and start again. I make it through the first three bars, before stumbling over a semi quaver.

'I'm sorry,' I say. 'I'm not sure what's going on.'

'Don't worry.' Miss Singer's voice is warm and reassuring.

Tears well at the bottom of my eyes. I try to blink them away.

'We've had a pretty intense beginning to your music classes here, especially when you have so much else to adjust to during your first term. I think we should finish for today. We can pick up again on Thursday.'

'But there are only ten days until we have to submit our piece.' My stomach twists.

'Right now, it's more important to rest and recharge our batteries. No one can play their best when they're tired.'

Miss Singer stops short of saying that I *look* tired.

'I think a break is a good idea,' agrees Jack, glancing my way. I'm sure he can see the tears glistening in my eyes. 'I've got some homework I really need to catch up on.'

'Make sure you get some time out, if you can,' says Miss Singer, collecting her port-com from the floor next to her chair.

'See you on Thursday,' says Jack.

The door slides open, and they disappear into the corridor.

I place my violin gently in its case. The room seems suddenly very quiet.

For the first time I can remember, I feel completely alone.

Logic

On Monday evening it starts raining heavily. There is nowhere quiet indoors for me and Mae to talk. Just before FOG, I find a hologram kitten curled up near my pillow. It stretches now and then, purring gently, only fading at lights out.

The next day there is a pause in the rain during Kin Space, so I head outside to the yard. I follow the wood-chip path around the school boundary. Silver birch leaves flutter past my head in the breeze. I wonder whether Chloe is in the garden, feeling the same breeze on her cheeks. Being outside makes me feel closer to home. I try not to think of Chloe inside, lying on the sofa, her face pale like before. What if there's nothing Mum and Dad can do to help? I walk as far as the enormous oaks near the gravel drive, then realize the light is beginning to fade, even though it's not very late.

Students aren't allowed out after dusk. I turn towards the entrance at the side of the school building. I don't want to go back inside. Part of me feels that if I stay out here long enough, I will come up with some answers, or at least a plan.

That night when the others fall asleep, I don't reach for my port-com.

I want to think. I want to think logically, like Violet. But logic doesn't seem enough when your family is in trouble. I see Mum and Dad, their faces tight with worry, Chloe on the sofa, pale and tired. I still can't see any pattern. Any solution.

If Mum and Dad had no credits to buy Chloe's medicine, would they steal them from someone else?

For the hundredth time, I play Violet's words back in my head. That cybercrime will be shut down immediately. Your cyber accounts and all online presence will be deactivated.

Could Mum and Dad have attempted a hack to try and fix things, with no idea how to cover their tracks, how to leave no trace?

An icy chill grips my heart. *Leave no trace.*

Perhaps Mum and Dad didn't do anything after all.

Perhaps I did.

The chill creeps slowly down my spine, as I remember.

The night I hacked the pharma system, I altered the tag on Dad's name. I wanted to locate an area which would reveal their purpose, show me what the tags were for. But then I didn't undo what I'd done. I left the system and rushed back to bed, so that I wouldn't be discovered. In the process, I made an error which would lead not to me—but to my parents. My hacking identity was protected. But I had changed Mum and Dad's account. I left a trace which could only incriminate them.

The next day Chloe's live-learning connection failed. A few days later, their port-watches shut down. There are no credits when they try to charge the car.

I sit up.

I need to do something. Now.

The sound of peaceful breathing, pushing softly against the silent room, doesn't reflect the whirlwind inside my head.

How could I be so stupid? So careless. I barely recognize the version of Jess I have become, she doesn't seem to be anything like the Jess from home. That Jess would never have made such a silly mistake.

I reach for the drawer where my port-com lies innocently on top of my folded T-shirts, then snatch my hand back. For the first time, it feels as if my port-com isn't the only place to search for answers. Desperation clears my head a little. It could take days to hack back in. To find a new weakness in the pharma security system. I have no idea how JP managed it in two days.

Maybe the only thing I can do is go home and find out what's really happening. Otherwise, how can I truly know what I must do to help?

That's it. I should figure out how I can get home. I glance down at my wrist to check the time. My port-watch is blank. It's been deactivated too.

Instinct

I'm still propped against my pillows as the birds begin to sing. Pale autumn sunrise filters around the edges of the blinds. One by one, the other girls stir. I head to the bathroom before they get up.

I tilt back my head and let warm water wash away the spaced-out feeling I have from being awake all night, the feeling of one day merging into the next. All showers last three minutes, to conserve water. I count down 180 seconds and, as the gentle spray clears my head, focus on the plan which began to form in the early hours of this morning.

Amongst Dad's books are other treasures. CDs—shiny disks which people used for playing music—and maps. Before port-watches, before we ran out of farmland and high fences were needed to protect intensive cropping, before 'approved pathways', people used to roam all over the countryside. They used paper maps which could unfold into huge sheets showing footpaths and streams, railway lines and towns. Mum taught me how to read contours. She taught me how to measure distance, and how to use a compass. Best of all, she would take me and Chloe on long walks, using only maps to find our way. She told us the routes were approved pathways, but now I realize that they can't have been. They were narrow tracks, often overgrown. We'd leave with our lunch in a backpack and walk for maybe nine or ten glorious kilometres.

There are maps here too. In the school archive library. If I can find the right one, then I can work out my way home. I can walk.

The shower stops, and I hear footsteps outside my cubicle.

I have lessons to go to.

One by one the other girls hurry towards the door, pulling on jumpers, bunching up hair to tie in pony-tails. Then for a few seconds, everything is still. For the first time in two days, it's just me and Mae in the dormitory. She rushes over to my bed, her hairbrush still in her hand.

'Jess, did you actually sleep last night?' she asks, eyes wide.

'Why?'

'I woke in the middle of the night, and you were just sitting up. Then this morning you were in the same position. Or did you fall asleep like that? It didn't look very comfortable.'

'No, I was awake,' I say quietly. The energy I felt in the shower has ebbed away.

'I can't go to breakfast until you've told me what's happening. Have you heard from your mum and dad? Come on,' Mae glances down at her port-watch, 'we don't have long.'

I tell Mae what I've done. That it's my fault.

She listens in silence, her green eyes fixed on mine.

I tell her that I have to go home. I have no other choice.

When I've finished, she shakes her head and blows air through her lips in a kind of low whistle.

'Jess, you know that Violet might have made up all that stuff about deleting people?'

I nod, remembering that Violet has no filter when she talks–she just says whatever she's thinking. 'But making up stuff is one thing Violet doesn't seem able to do.'

'I need to think about this,' says Mae. 'I can't think properly on an empty stomach. But, Jess, you shouldn't go home.'

'Why not?'

'I don't know. I'm not like Violet, I can't give you ruthless logic. It's just a feeling. Anyway, you can't go anywhere before Friday, can you?' When I don't answer, she adds, 'People will notice you've gone immediately—when you don't turn up for lessons. Come on.' She glances at her port-watch again. 'Breakfast is almost over. I'll give you some better answers when I've eaten.'

Plan

The bell hums, signalling the end of plant science. I stand up to leave.

'Jessica.'

Miss Ali beckons me back into the classroom. I let the other kids go by, then walk over to her desk, wondering whether it's something to do with my classwork on Monday. She glances at her screen, then at me.

'I have a message here, requesting that you go to the principal's office.' She pauses. Perhaps waiting for me to explain what it's about. 'She would like to see you straight away.'

I nod. 'During break?'

'Yes, I believe so.'

My mouth feels dry. I wish I did know what it's about.

I knock on the door to the principal's office. She welcomes me inside, smiling. I sit in the comfortable armchair next to hers.

'Jessica,' she keeps smiling, 'very regretfully, the school has encountered some credit issues for supplementary elements of your schooling.' I'm guessing that means food and dormitory. 'But the real problem is that no one has been able to contact your parents to discuss it. If they are refusing to communicate with the school, then sadly the school has no choice but to send you home until matters are resolved.'

As she speaks, I have the strangest sensation that I'm watching myself, sitting in the comfortable chair. That I've somehow split in two, and the real me is floating nearby. The real me is continuing life as normal, the real me can port-com their family whenever they like. Everything is fine.

'We will arrange for the school transport to take you home on Friday afternoon, to coincide with any other weekend student transfers.'

'Yes, of course,' I hear myself saying.

I am to take a small bag, but leave the majority of my belongings here, as she feels confident things can be sorted out and I will return to full-contact education again very soon.

I close the door behind me. If my parents really have been deleted, they can't connect to anything. Now my port-watch is dead, it feels like I'm being deleted too. The only way I can access anything digital, fix anything, is through the school's shared network. If I'm not here, I'll be locked out of that as well. I have to be somewhere I can connect. Whilst listening to the principal talk, I realized that Mae is right. I can't go home yet.

I arrive a few minutes late for programming. The teacher doesn't seem to mind, but I sense Violet's eyes on me. I wish she wasn't always watching.

When the bell goes for lunch, I rush to find Mae. It's still dry outside, but the grass under the oak tree is wet.

'Let's go down here,' I point to the woodchip path winding along the edge of the playing field. 'Then at least no one can hear what we're saying.'

She nods.

'The principal asked to see me.'

Mae spins round. 'No! Does she know something?'

'Shhhh,' I hiss. 'She told me that my parents' credits have stopped, and it hasn't been possible to talk to them about it. They want to send me home until the issue has been resolved.'

'*They* want to send *you* home. When?'

'Friday afternoon.'

Mae nods again. We walk in silence towards the spinney of oak trees. Their topmost branches shiver in the wind, scattering orange-brown leaves into the air.

As I wait for Mae to tell me what I should do, the cold feeling begins to creep down my spine again. She doesn't know what I should do, and neither do I.

'Perhaps I just have to try and hack back into the system. That's where it all began, after all,' I say.

'Surely that's a good reason not to do it again? Anyway, you only have two days. You said yourself that even three days wouldn't be long enough.'

We walk in silence again.

'What about your friend?' asks Mae. 'Can Finn help?'

I know Finn would try to help me if he could. If he knew. Perhaps he's already wondering why he hasn't heard from me or Chloe. Although he always seems so busy, perhaps he hasn't realized yet. But Finn isn't a programmer. He isn't a hacker. And right now, that's the kind of help I need most.

'Finn doesn't know,' I say.

Mae looks at me, her head tilted slightly in thought.

'He doesn't know about your mum and dad?'

'He doesn't know about Mum and Dad or the hacking stuff.'

The path loops around a bench, then heads back towards school.

I slow down. By the time we reach the yard, it will be time to go back inside, but I don't want to. Not until I have a plan. A new plan.

'Wait!' says Mae, she takes my arm. 'Where is Finn's school?'

'It's about half an hour from home I think.'

'I mean, how far from here?'

'I don't know. Our school is in the opposite direction from home to Finn's. So maybe an hour, an hour and a half from here.'

'By transport?'

'Yes.'

We've both stopped walking. I glance over at the yard. Students are filtering towards the door, ready for the bell.

'Can you go to Finn's school?'

I stare at Mae blankly.

'Honestly, Jess, for someone so clever, sometimes you are really slow to catch on. Can you go to Finn's school, so that you have somewhere to use your port-com—so that you have time to do whatever it is you need to do—without being sent home? You can connect to *his* school's network.'

'But I might not be able to *do* anything. And

someone will work out that I didn't go home on the transport, that I've actually run away, and I might make everything even worse.'

'Worse than it is?'

'What if I get Finn into trouble, too? None of this would have happened if I hadn't messed up in the first place.'

'I guess that's possible,' Mae agrees. 'But the idea would be that no one knows you're there—at least until you've finished. Why don't you ask him what he thinks?'

I hear the low humming of the bell.

'But my port-watch doesn't work.'

'Use mine.'

The last few students have left the yard. Only Mae and I are still outside.

'If I use your port-watch, how will Finn know it's actually me? He might think someone's playing a joke. Especially if I ask to come and see him.'

The heavy feeling creeps back. Mae looks anxiously towards the door. I'm about to say that we should keep thinking, try to find a different solution, when I remember the code. Finn's code for Chloe. There's no way anyone would know about that except for me, Finn and Chloe.

'Pass me your port-watch,' I say.

Mae frowns, confused by my change of heart, but unclips her watch and passes it to me. I don't have time to explain.

I know the code, but I haven't used it for a few days. I try to concentrate, speaking each letter softly into Mae's port-watch, translating directly from the message in my head:

Finn it's Jess. No time to explain. I need your help. Can I come and see you? Soon, maybe Saturday. My port-watch is broken. Reply to this one.

'Jess,' Mae whispers, 'Mrs Drew is coming.'

'*Send,*' I whisper, and place the port-watch in Mae's outstretched hand. We hurry past Mrs Drew and through the open door.

I have a plan.

Distance

The archive library is shadowy and silent. There are no large windows through which natural light floods in—unlike the rest of school. Low-energy lamps line the walls, casting a soft glow which won't damage the items stored here. I pass rows of cabinets filled with books of different shapes and sizes. Some have hard covers, but most of them look like paperbacks. I keep going, until I reach the final cabinet, at the back of the room. This is where Miss Campbell, the geography teacher, said I would find the maps. When I told her I was researching a local history project in my free time, she granted me a two-week security pass.

The maps are stored side-on. I can't work out how they've been organized, so I ease one out, and look at the back to see which area it covers. It's miles from here but shows me the reference number for the map I need. I slide another from the row below, then another, until I find the right one. The cover is orange, the same as the maps which Mum used, the ones which show contours and rivers, roads and houses.

I take it to a large table by the wall. The thin white paper crackles as I open it out, just like the maps at home. It reminds me of the day Finn and I discovered we would be going to different schools. At first we thought there must have been a mistake so Mum double-checked. Later that day, she invited Finn inside for lunch. After we'd cleared everything away, she unfolded a map on the kitchen table. Some of the roads and towns had moved or grown larger, but using her port-watch, we were able to work out where my school would be, and where Finn's school would be. Tracing a line with my finger, from one to the other, made me feel so much better—like they were connected, somehow.

I draw a line with my finger again, then I count the squares from this school to Finn's. As the crow flies, it's about seventeen kilometres. If I walked at the same speed as when I was hiking with Mum, that would take about four hours. I feel a flicker of hope. I can definitely walk that far—at least in daylight I can, when I know the route.

Filtering through the stillness of the archive room, is the low hum of the dinner bell. Without my port-watch I feel lost. I hate not knowing what time it is.

My stomach lurches. Not because I'm hungry. I realize I've missed music practice with Jack and Miss Singer.

As quickly as I can, I re-fold the map and tuck it under my T-shirt. Nothing is supposed to leave this room, but I can't scan the map without my port-watch.

The corridor is filling with students making their way to the dining hall. I walk in the opposite direction, towards the music room. I don't have my violin with me. I'm not even sure what I'm going to say, how I'll explain arriving an hour late, whether they'll spot the map. I just want to see Jack and Miss Singer.

I arrive at the door, out of breath. I press my face against the window, but the room is dark. They've already gone.

Ally

'What does it say?' Mae whispers.

There are other people in the common room, but it's raining again, and there's nowhere else to go.

'Wait a minute.' I read the jumble of letters back to myself.

Yes, come here, I decipher slowly. *Will help if can. Wait in hut by football field. Will keep checking x Finn*

'He'll be waiting for me. He said come.' I blink away the tears which are rising up.

Mae nods.

'So tomorrow, after lessons, school transport will be waiting outside,' she whispers, her eyes blazing with excitement.

'Yes,' I say, wondering how she can feel excited, when so much can go wrong.

'If it's straight after lessons end, there'll be lots of people walking around.'

I nod, wishing Mae would get to the point.

'So, no one would notice if I went out to tell the driver that you're ill and have to stay in quarantine this weekend.' She smiles triumphantly, eyes sparkling. 'He'll just leave without you. As long as you don't let anyone see you after that, then no one will realize what's happened. We'll need to make up a reason for me to go home though.'

'What do you mean?'

'You didn't think I was going to let you do this on your own, did you?'

'Won't it seem suspicious if we're both away?'

'Why? When there's no reason to be suspicious? My mum can't help it if that's when she happens to have her birthday.'

'Your mum's birthday is—' I stop mid-sentence when Mae buries her face in her hands. 'It's not really your mum's birthday, is it?'

Mae shakes her head. 'No. You're getting better at this.'

I can't help letting some of Mae's enthusiasm rub off on me. She makes everything seem possible. But it doesn't change the fact that I might mess things up for her, too.

'Running away is definitely against school rules,' I say. 'They might not let you back. I have to go, but you have a choice.'

'And I choose to come with you,' she smiles. 'But,' Mae lowers her voice so that I can barely hear, 'you have to act normally until it's time to go.'

'Then people will definitely know that something is wrong,' I smile back.

'That's more like it,' says Mae. 'Let's go to the dorm. I had something delivered this morning.'

The dormitory is empty. Mae slides open the drawer beneath her bed. Lying on top of her clothes is something smooth and black. I reach down and turn it over. There are two padded straps on one side and a small clip on the other.

'Backpack,' she says. 'And look.' Beneath the backpack are two flasks and a square packet, half the size of a book. 'Flasks and energy bars. Violet's not the only one with a Rapid Drone Delivery account.'

'This is amazing,' I gasp. Before I can say anything more, the door swishes open and Violet walks in. She heads straight to her bed without looking our way. I slide Mae's drawer gently shut.

It must be obvious that we've just stopped talking.

'Have they chosen the team for hockey yet?' I ask, realizing how fake I must sound.

'No, next week. It's going to be inter-year. There aren't enough players from S1.'

I nod, but I'm not really listening. I'm thinking about other things we need to take. The map inside my trunk. My port-com. It doesn't roll up like everyone else's. It's not very heavy, but it won't fit in Mae's backpack.

I reach for Mae's wrist and tap a message on her port-watch.

We're going to need a bigger bag. And a compass.

'Normal'

Mae said the most important thing is to act normally. The more I think about acting normally, the less sure I am of what that means. It's almost impossible to concentrate. I try to focus on what the teachers say, but every time I hear a drone overhead, I wonder if it's carrying a larger backpack, then I think about Finn, and about Chloe, and whether taking more risks is going to make things better or much much worse.

I realize that I'm staring blankly at my screen again, when the bell hums, marking the end of history and of lessons for me today. Perhaps for ever.

I weave my way around the other students in the corridor. I need to collect my things from the dorm and be out of sight before the transport leaves. I wish we'd had more time to plan. Surely we've forgotten something important.

I'm walking so fast, I barely notice a voice behind, calling my name. I spin round. It's Violet.

'Jess, can I talk to you?' She is hurrying down the corridor towards me.

'I'm, err, a bit late. Can we talk later?'

A shadow of something passes over Violet's face. I can't tell if she's annoyed or upset. Almost immediately, the shadow passes.

'Later. OK,' she says, slowing down.

When I reach the dormitory I hurry over to my bed. I know the others will return from their lessons any minute.

Lying inside my drawer, on top of my port-com, is a smooth black bundle—a backpack, larger than the one Mae had yesterday.

'*Thank you,*' I whisper.

There is also a flask, energy bars and a compass. I slide them all inside the backpack. I lift the lid of my trunk and take out the map. Beneath is Dad's small grey book. I hold it in my hands for a few seconds, then place the map and the book in the backpack too.

The dormitory door opens and Eve enters, speaking softly into her port-watch. Nyla follows closely behind, her head craned forwards as if she's trying to catch what Eve is saying.

I will have to pass them to reach the door. I tug at one of my jumpers, folded neatly in the drawer—a large grey hoodie. I wrap it around the backpack. Now it just looks like a large item of clothing, heaped on the bedspread.

Eve and Nyla are watching something—a small brown creature—scampering across one of the chairs. I guess Eve had been ordering a hologram. While they are distracted, I gather the bundle beneath my arm and head to the door.

I agreed to wait for Mae in the archive library, where no one is likely to see me.

I'm grateful to step away from the bustling corridor, into the peaceful silence. I place my grey bundle on one of the empty desks.

I had planned to pull up a chair and maybe find a book to read while I wait for Mae. That would also provide an excuse for my presence in a restricted room. Instead, I find myself walking back through the door, and into the corridor. I turn left, towards the music room.

I need to see Jack and Miss Singer. Explain to them that I have to go away for a few days—for family reasons, but I hope to be back soon. That I'm sorry to let them down.

Even though I'm late, when I peer through the door, I see Miss Singer but no Jack. He's always on time.

'Ah, Jess!' she smiles as I enter the room, then when I don't come any further, her smile fades a little.

'Is everything OK? I'm sorry, Jack won't be joining us today. He's been a little poorly.'

'Oh no. Is he all right now? I mean—will he be OK?'

'He's in the medical wing, and I think he's feeling much better. He just needs some rest.'

I nod. 'Of course.' My voice is far quieter than I meant it to be, and a little shakier.

'Don't worry,' Miss Singer adds. 'We'll still have time to prepare—just about!'

I nod again. She must have noticed I'm not carrying my violin.

She rests her port-screen in her lap. 'Perhaps we should wait until Jack is better before we practise the piece again. Shall we meet on Monday, instead?'

'Yes, I think that's sensible,' I say, my voice even shakier than before. 'Monday.'

Everything I had planned to say evaporates. I wonder why it's so much harder to let someone down when you have to do it in person.

Risk

In a daze, I walk straight past the archive room, and have to retrace my steps a few metres. There is no sign of Mae. She should be here by now.

I didn't need to go to the music room. It was stupid. Now I might have messed everything up before we've even left the building.

The seconds speed by, and she doesn't appear. For about the millionth time, I wish I had my port-watch.

The door swishes and I look up, but it's not Mae. It's Miss Campbell. My heart begins to thump.

'I thought it was you,' she says. 'Did you find what you were looking for? Maps, wasn't it?' She glances at my grey bundle, out of place on the sleek, smooth desktop.

'Yes, thank you. I—' I try desperately to think of a reason why I might just be sitting here. 'I'm waiting for Mae. I wanted to show them to her too,' I say.

'Wonderful,' she beams. 'Just make sure you put them back in the right place. And keep the table nice and clean.' She gives my bundle a meaningful look.

I place it on the chair next to me. 'Of course, we'll be very careful,' I smile.

'Ah, Mae,' says Miss Campbell stepping aside. 'I'm sure you would like to get started.'

Mae's eyes flick to me. I smile and nod.

'Yes. That's right,' she replies. As the door slides shut behind Miss Campbell, she whispers, 'Where *were* you? I had to do another lap of the school. Three teachers walked past while I was outside the archive room.'

'I'm sorry, I got held up.'

'Let's hope Miss Campbell doesn't see the principal in the next few minutes. You're supposed to be on your way home already.' She pauses. 'The transport has just left. When I told the driver you were ill, he couldn't get away fast enough. Well? What are we waiting for?' she adds, as if we're about to leave for a picnic.

I wonder whether she's taking our plan seriously enough.

'Are you sure you want to do this?' I ask.

Mae stares at me. I can't work out what her expression means. I spot that she's wearing her backpack. I barely noticed it next to her black top.

'You don't want me to come?'

'That's not what I said. We're basically running away from school, which is totally forbidden. I don't even know if I'm going to be able to fix things. There's no point in both of us getting into trouble. Perhaps I should go on my own.'

'No way. You got yourself into this mess, and I'm going to help to get you out. That's what friends are for.'

A strange scrabbling noise begins, somewhere near the ceiling. We both look up.

'Rain,' I say.

'Well that changes everything,' Mae smiles. 'You didn't say it would be raining.' She looks at her port-watch. 'OK. Let's go.'

Fake

As we approach the exit, raindrops patter against the window. Beyond the yard, the field appears blurred in the downpour. No one will be doing sport in this weather. The risk of chest infection or injury is too high. I pull on my raincoat, over the top of my back-pack. Mae does the same.

'Ready?' I ask quietly. She nods, and we step outside.

We skirt the edges of the school building. The windows overlooking the yard are all classrooms, which should be empty now. We follow the boundary of the field, avoiding a more direct route through the leaf-strewn grass. Cold wind spatters rain across my cheeks and creeps beneath the edges of my hood.

Past the field is a ditch and a low wooden fence. I jump over the ditch and straddle the fence, turning to make sure that Mae is following.

Leaving school feels too easy. But then I guess they don't expect anyone will run away.

I blink raindrops from my eyelashes and peer ahead to a small group of trees. I need a sheltered spot to check the map.

The trees offer some protection from the rain, but many of their leaves have already dropped. I beckon to Mae, then unzip my waterproof and pass it to her, so that she can hold it over my head and shield the paper from raindrops.

I place the compass above the square which contains our school.

'How does that thing work?' asks Mae, her voice muffled above my waterproof. 'Satellites?'

'The earth's magnetism.'

'Seriously?'

'We need to head this way,' I point slightly to the right, 'for two kilometres. Then I'll check again. The route looks mostly flat.'

'What about approved pathways?' asks Mae.

'Approved pathways didn't exist when these maps were made,' I say, rain dripping from the end of my nose as I carefully fold the map and slip it inside the backpack.

'Don't we need that?' asks Mae.

'I can use the compass bearing for now. But I do need

your port-watch. I have to send a message to Finn, so that he knows I've left.'

Mae pushes her wrist towards me. I spell out *8w fc 9tc—on my way.*

I haven't told him there will be two of us.

We carry on, through the trees, towards an area of brambles beyond.

My legs are damp from the knee down.

'Do you think we'll get there before dark?' asks Mae.

'It will be dusk soon, and dark not long after that.'

'I didn't buy torches!' she cries.

'It's better to walk without them. Let your eyes adjust.'

As Mae stomps along beside me, I realize how glad I am that she's here, that I don't have to do this alone.

The ground is carpeted with leaves, shining wet. Their earthy smell reminds me of sitting in the tree-house with Finn and Chloe. Wrapped in coats and hats, watching the steam rise from cups of hot chocolate.

'So what's Finn like?' Mae asks, reading my mind.

I wonder how to describe him. I've never had to do it before. He's just Finn.

'He has slightly crazy hair.' I pause while we clamber over a mossy tree trunk.

'Is that all?'

'He talks a lot. He's kind, especially to Chloe. He's the one who came up with the secret message code, so that she didn't miss us too much.' I brush rainwater from my face. At least now that we're walking, I don't feel cold. 'I've known him for as long as I can remember. I guess he feels a bit like family.'

'Does he know what's going on?'

'No.' I think about the voices in the background when we port-com. How Finn always needs to be in two places at once. 'I find it harder to talk with him—virtually.'

'I guess we're lucky,' says Mae.

'Why?'

'Lucky to have *real* friends before starting school.'

'Aren't live-learning friends, *real* friends? Or the ones you meet on ROOM?'

'What about filters and morph-tech? You can change the way you look entirely. Be someone else entirely, and no one would know for sure. It depends on what you mean by real.'

'Don't people pretend a bit when you meet them, too? You didn't tell me about your mum's school. I didn't tell you about hacking.'

'That's true. But it's harder to hide the things you'd prefer to keep hidden when you meet someone for real. You can't just show them the bits you like.'

'At least with ROOM you have thousands of ROOMmates to choose from and you can "kick them out" when you want. They never borrow your hair-brush either.'

There is a cracking sound from somewhere behind. Like a branch snapping.

We both spin round. It's hard to focus with rain dripping from my eyelashes, but I see only trees, and beneath them a tangle of bramble and bracken.

We keep walking. Perhaps it was an old branch falling. Weakened by the rain.

Mae glances at her port-watch. 'Only 16,200 metres left to go,' she says.

'Approximately,' I add.

It feels hard to chat like we were a few moments ago. We are listening now instead. There is a strange prickling sensation at the back of my neck. I want to turn round, to keep checking, but I don't want to make Mae nervous.

As dusk falls, it's difficult to see very far ahead.

There is another cracking sound. We spin round again, but this time we don't stand still. We keep moving, slowly backing away, ready to run.

'What do you think it is?' whispers Mae.

'Maybe a deer,' I say softly.

Rain drips from my hood, pattering onto my chest.

I'm about to turn round, when there is a rustling noise and something lurches into the path in front of us. Mae lets out a small cry.

I step backwards, my heart pounding.

The thing on the path begins to move. It gets to its feet and looks at us.

The thing on the path is Violet.

There is a smear of mud on her cheek. Strands of wet hair are plastered to her face and she looks as if she's about to cry.

'What the—!' is all Mae manages to say. Her mouth hangs open.

I look past Violet, to the path beyond, to see who she's with.

'Which teacher did you tell?' I ask her. 'Or did you go straight to the principal? Tell her how you've been spying on us, that we were going to run away?'

Someone is bound to be close behind Violet, in earshot, but I don't care any more. The enormity of what her arrival means is dawning on me. We will have to go back to school. Then I will be sent home. So will Mae.

Violet brushes the wet hair from her eyes.

She doesn't look upset any more. She doesn't look guilty either. Violet is scowling at me. With a shock, I realize she is angry.

I wonder what it might take for her to understand what she's done. To feel bad about it.

'What's in it for you?' I snap. 'Just the fun of watching us being marched back to school?'

For a few moments, Violet says nothing. I begin to think she won't answer at all.

Then she breathes in and out, loudly, as if she can't believe she has to deal with people like me and Mae.

'I didn't tell anybody,' she says quietly. 'Although *you* might as well have. You made it so obvious that you were planning to leave.'

'Then—' I frown. 'What are you doing here?'

She stares at me as if I'm completely stupid, or completely mad, or both. Several seconds pass, as if she's waiting for me to work it out, then she says, still staring, 'I've come to help you.'

I close my eyes, for a second, feeling the tension drain from my shoulders. I'm not sure I can deal with any more surprises. I feel my cheeks burning too, despite the freezing rain. Because, whatever else I might think about her, Violet doesn't seem able to lie.

I have a sudden urge to laugh. It's partly relief, but it's also the way she's looking at me. Her expression is so serious, but she is wearing something which looks like a black spacesuit. Her knees are caked in mud, and her hair is making a break for freedom from beneath her shiny black hood.

'Help us how?' asks Mae.

'Help Jess,' Violet clarifies, 'to restore her parents.'

'But I thought you said it was impossible?'

'Then what are *you* doing here?' she replies.

There's no point in hiding the truth from Violet. Not now.

'The principal wanted to send me home. If I go home, there will be no way for me to sort things out. I was supposed to be on the transport this afternoon.'

'I know,' says Violet. 'So where are you going instead?'

'To see my friend. He can help me.'

'Is he a hacker? Like you?'

I feel the colour drain from my face. 'No. But he'll find somewhere for us to hide, somewhere with a network and power I can use, while I try to figure out how to fix this.'

'So you know how to fix it? You have a plan?'

'Leave her alone,' says Mae. 'What do you suggest? That she should just go home and cease to "exist" too? She's the only chance her family has.'

This time I don't try and get Mae to be quiet.

Her voice is drowning out the truth. That I don't have a plan.

'Have you finished?' asks Violet, rain dripping from the end of her nose.

'No, I haven't finished,' says Mae. 'What's *your* plan? You said you're here to help, but unless you can rescue Jess's family using ROOM, then I don't feel you have much to offer. At least Jess knows how to get inside computer systems. How to hack.'

'What makes you think she's the only one at our school who can do that?' says Violet. 'Haven't you noticed how good everyone is at programming?'

'Not everyone,' says Mae.

'More than average.'

'Well I don't know what's average.'

'Well I do. My dad is head of security. I know more about cyber safety than the teachers.'

'If you know so much, why bother coming to school at all?'

'Because I'm smart enough to realize I don't know everything, and the teachers here are the best.'

Violet's words begin to filter through.

'Wait—stop,' I say.

Mae and Violet both turn to look at me.

'What do you mean, haven't we noticed how good everyone is? Why are they so good? What's special about this school?'

'Finally, an intelligent question,' says Violet.

Violet's outline is becoming a little hazy as her black spacesuit melts into the gloom. She doesn't answer straight away. For a few seconds, I hear only the steady drip of rain.

'My father—'

'*My father,*' mimics Mae.

Violet rolls her eyes.

'Let's hear what she has to say.' I turn to Mae. 'She's here now.' I don't mention it, but Mae must have noticed that no one has arrived to drag us back to school, yet.

Violet looks from me to Mae, then begins again.

'My father says the only way to beat cybercriminals is to know who they are, to know how they work. But even better than that, is to get them to work for you instead.'

'Fascinating,' says Mae. 'But I don't see what that has to do with our school.'

'The best cybercriminals are always brilliant programmers,' says Violet. 'My father's company uses live-learning data to identify who they are, and they come to schools like ours, where they can be monitored, and later, recruited. Parents are unaware these schools are different. In fact, the only clue is the absence of your live-learning cohort. Of course, some students are less exceptional than others.' She glances at Mae. 'The most gifted are assigned cyber-minders. It's a good way of keeping tabs.'

'Cyber-minders?' I say, my head spinning.

'Yes, cybersecurity agents who can help develop your skills, while keeping an eye on what you're up to. The trick is making a good partnership. Understanding what kind of hacks might interest them. It's very hard to do well.' She hesitates.

'And how do you know that?' I ask, an icy feeling creeping along my spine.

'I'm a cyber-minder myself.'

Despite the water running down my face, my mouth feels suddenly dry.

'You call me Violet,' she pauses, 'but you also call me JP.'

The ground seems to tilt a little beneath my feet. I put my arm on Mae's shoulder to steady myself.

'What is it? What's going on?' says Mae.

'I didn't know it was you,' says Violet, looking straight at me. 'Not when we started school. All I knew was that Dad had assigned me someone my age. He said you'd been caught immediately, but when he discovered you were only twelve, he thought you had a talent worth sparing. He thought we could develop each other's skills. Then when I got here, I noticed you were using your port-com at night.

That was the only time I got messages. Then, one night, I saw you.'

Slowly, I begin to nod.

Mae has been listening in silence for the last few minutes. She shrugs my hand from her shoulder, looking from Violet to me and back, her palms facing up as if she's holding two invisible bags of sugar. She sighs.

'Will someone please tell me what's going on?'

Dark

We walk in single file. Me, Mae and Violet.

I tried to explain to Mae, how Violet was also someone called JP, how she knows about hacking—knows everything. But my own head is a whirlwind of truth and illusion, real and virtual.

Only Violet seems unperturbed as we trudge through the undergrowth in the failing light.

I'm glad. Because I'm beginning to understand how much I need her. I just don't know if I can trust her. Yet.

Darkness falls softly, like the rain. The wooded area peters out, its boundary marked by a barbed wire fence. We lift the wire and crawl beneath. Violet is terrified of scratching herself, of the wound becoming infected, so I take off my jumper and wrap it around the sharp spikes. By the time she has wriggled through, the sleeves are patchworked with ragged holes, and soaking wet. The fence continues along one side of a road. On the opposite side, a barrier made from heavy-duty recycled plastic rises several metres. The type of barrier farmers use to keep people away from their crops. There's no way we can climb over the top.

I tug the compass from my pocket.

'What's that?' asks Violet suspiciously.

'It tells us which way we need to go.'

She shines her port-watch on it, frowning.

I unzip my backpack and take out the map.

'Paper?' asks Violet.

'It's a map. Also tells us which way to go.'

'I thought we were going to your friend's school, not back in time,' says Violet.

'Port-watches only show approved routes. We need to know what's in between.'

I trace my finger across the squares in the map. 'We've walked three kilometres.'

'It's already half-past six. We're going quite slowly,' says Mae, a slight edge to her voice.

The rain has slowed to a drizzle, but the wind feels stronger, tugging at the map as I fold it back up.

My stomach growls. Normally we would have eaten dinner by now.

'I hope it's not going to be much further. I have to be back before everyone gets up tomorrow,' says

Violet. 'Or else my father will have half the country out looking for me.'

I feel my chest tighten.

'Violet, we're not even a quarter of the way there. There's no way we can make it back to school by tomorrow morning. Not unless we turn around now.'

'You mean, you came after us with no plan to explain where you'd gone?' says Mae. 'Now everyone will be chasing us before we've even got to Finn's school!'

Violet says nothing.

I close my eyes for a second, then take a deep breath.

'Well, there's nothing we can do. We can't go back.'

'I told Eve I had a headache and was going to the medical wing,' says Violet quietly.

'Well, that should buy us some time.' I try to keep my voice steady. 'But we need to walk faster.'

I'm starting to feel there's no way this can work. That I am dragging Mae, Finn and now Violet into the mess I have created.

I try to concentrate on what we're doing right now, to stop the tight sensation in my chest from spreading.

'OK, we can't go over the fence, so we have to follow this road,' I point, 'then join a footpath after another few kilometres. The footpath probably hasn't been used for years, but it is much more direct. There's less chance of being seen, too.'

We cross the road. Me, followed by Violet, then Mae. Since we stopped, I feel much colder. The moisture from my jumper has seeped through to my T-shirt. Wet socks cling to my toes. After an hour or so, I'm still wet, but I've begun to warm up a little.

The moon has risen, creating a silvery glow within the clouds. There is just enough light to see by.

My stomach twists with hunger, but I don't mention it. I don't want to stop again.

I think of Finn, waiting, trying to figure out what's going on. He will be looking out for a lone figure, not three.

'Come on!' Mae urges from a few metres behind.

I turn round to see Violet crouching down, her back to the fence.

'We won't be there before dawn if you just sit there!'

I take a few steps towards them.

'Mae,' I say quietly, 'I don't think Violet is as used to walking outside as we are.' I hesitate. 'Perhaps you could give her a break?'

Mae glares at me, her face ghostly in the pale grey moonlight. But when she speaks again, her tone is gentler.

'Violet, it's almost midnight. We have to keep moving. Here, have one of these.' She rummages inside her tiny backpack. 'We should have eaten them ages ago.' Mae passes a small packet to each of us.

'What's this?' Violet asks. Even her voice sounds weary.

'Energy bar. Food.'

'Oh.' She unzips a pouch in the side of her spacesuit and pulls out several crumpled black bags. 'Do you have some water?'

Mae hands her a flask.

Violet tips a little into one of the bags and then shakes it. 'I saw these advertised on ROOM. They come free with the safari décor package.'

Mae coughs, as if trying to clear her throat, but says nothing.

Violet passes a bag to me and prepares another for Mae. 'Tug the top, and the spoon will fold out.'

I do as I'm instructed. The crumpled bag feels strangely substantial. I dig my spoon inside and place a small scoop of paste in my mouth. There is an explosion of flavour. Chicken and roast potatoes with gravy. Although it looks smooth, the paste needs chewing, like real food.

'Made with 3D molecular food printing. It gives a much better texture when rehydrated,' Violet says, passing a bag to Mae.

Mae eats in silence until the bag seems to be empty. 'OK,' she says, 'these are way better than my energy bars.'

While Violet finishes hers, I take out the compass.

'Fourteen kilometres down,' says Mae.

The fenced-off farmland has added about a kilometre to our journey, but ahead is a ridge too steep for farming. If we follow the contours, then the final few kilometres will be more direct.

'We need to leave the road again in a few hundred metres. There should be a way through between the fields.'

'I'm ready.' Violet gets to her feet. Her face is pale, but the molecular printed survival rations have given us all a little more energy.

Before we can start walking, I hear a low humming noise. It gets steadily louder.

'Transport,' hisses Mae.

I grasp Violet's arm and pull her towards the brambles sprawling up the side of the fence. She doesn't resist. She seems to be trembling.

'Face away from it. We're all wearing black. They might not see us,' I say.

We lean into the brambles, thorns grasping at our clothes. The orange-brown foliage lights up as the transport draws level, plunging into darkness moments later. Transports are so quiet. I can't tell if it has stopped. After a few seconds, I can't bear it any longer. I turn my head to look down the road. It's empty. They've gone, but we can't know if they saw us. Three people walking at midnight on an unapproved route would be worth reporting.

'Do you think they'll come back?' asks Violet, her voice shaking.

'I don't think anyone will bother sending police drones out for us tonight. It's too windy for a start. Let's keep moving,' I add, sounding more confident than I feel.

After the bright lights of the transport, my eyes must readjust to the pale moonlit ground.

I step from the road into a dark, overgrown gully. Brambles and branches catch on my leggings and the wind whips around my hood. I think about Chloe at home and wonder whether she's asleep, whether she's OK. I wonder what happens when your family has been deleted. How long can you survive when you no longer exist?

Trust

'What's that?' Mae calls softly from somewhere behind me. I stop walking and squint through the trees. A dark shape rises above the canopy.

I pull the compass from my pocket and point it towards the shape. My whole body is aching. My socks are rubbing against my toes. We've been walking for six or seven hours. I wait, as the arrow spins round to north. The shape lines up perfectly with the course we have been following.

'That must be it,' I say. 'Finn's school.'

My heart starts pumping faster. Three people will be far more difficult to hide than one.

I turn to Mae and Violet. Violet is leaning forwards, resting one hand on her knee. Her eyes sparkle in the moonlight. I realize that she's trying not to cry.

'We just need to find the sports field,' I say softly. 'It can't be far. Maybe we should have some energy bars when we stop, too.'

Mae pats Violet on the shoulder. 'This has been epic. I really didn't think you'd manage it,' she smiles.

I think she's trying to be kind.

Violet turns to Mae. She takes a deep breath. 'Let's find this field then.'

As we get closer, I can see that this school building is nothing like ours. Ours is low, and wooden, the gently pitching roof glazed with solar panels. This building looks ancient. It's made of stone or brick, with sloping roofs and gables. It's just like one of the boarding schools in Dad's old books.

A fence looms from the shadows obscuring the building behind. It's lower than the farmer's fences, but higher than my head.

'I think we can get over it,' says Mae. 'Better than walking down the main drive.'

'I can't,' says Violet. 'I can't climb over. I don't even think I can walk any more.'

'If Mae climbs over, I can make a step with my hands and push you up, then Mae can help you down the other side.'

I feel a pulse of energy. Finn is nearby, somewhere.

'I'm not sure I can take another step either,' Mae

says to Violet, 'but I'm going to have a go. We've come this far.'

Violet looks unsure. Mae places her hands on the top of the fence and begins to haul herself up. There is a soft thump and a rustle of leaves.

'Ouch! There are nettles or something. It got my hand.'

'Shhh,' I hiss.

Violet grabs my arm. 'What are nettles?'

'Don't worry. They're harmless. Can give a bit of a sting though,' I whisper.

'Put your foot here.' I lace my fingers together, making a cup shape with my hands.

Violet moves closer. She places her right foot where my fingers link. Her shoe is wet and muddy, but I try not to flinch.

'One, two three.'

Violet rises, hooking her arms over the top.

I give another push, until she is draped like a piece of clothing. 'Lift one leg, then swing the other up after it,' I call, as quietly as I can.

I hear a soft whimper and she slides gently to the other side. There is a gasp, and the sound of twigs breaking.

The energy I felt a few minutes ago has ebbed away. My arms burn as finally I pull myself over, landing on my feet next to Mae. Violet is on the ground, rubbing her arm. 'Do you think it might be broken?' she asks, eyes wide with fright.

'If it was broken, you wouldn't be able to rub it,' I whisper. 'Let's get to the hut and I can have a proper look.' I offer my hand for her to take with her good arm.

Through the gloom, I can make out what looks like an enormous door towards the centre of the building.

'I think this must be the front. The playing field will be at the back,' I say, thinking of the illustrations in Dad's books. 'Let's follow the fence round.'

We move in single file, Violet still clutching her arm.

Wind has scattered the rain clouds. The moon casts an eery, silvery light across the school walls. Even in the shadows, I feel exposed. There is no way to explain creeping around the grounds in the early hours of the morning.

As we draw level with the edge of the building, Violet lets out a tiny scream. Seconds later, someone grabs my arm. I feel my heart thumping.

A figure steps in front of me. A figure with scruffy hair.

'Jess!' Finn says softly.

Without stopping to think, I throw my arms around him, a sob rising in my chest. A familiar voice, a voice from home, makes what is happening feel so much more real.

'Jess, you're OK.' It's a statement. Finn pushes my shoulders away to look me in the face. 'I have no idea what's going on, but I'm going to help.'

There is a sniff from nearby.

I spin round to see Violet leaning, exhausted, against Mae's shoulder.

'I should have told you I wouldn't be alone. Mae, Violet, this is Finn.'

Team

'Start at the beginning,' Finn whispers.

We are sitting on the floor of a storeroom, next to the kitchen, not far from the bathroom where Finn had left a window open for us to climb through. My socks and our coats are hanging from some shelves to dry, although Violet's spacesuit didn't seem wet in the first place.

'We're miles from the dormitories, but one of the teachers is always on duty. So we need to be quiet,' he adds.

Violet nibbles at an energy bar, her eyes fixed on Finn. Mae finished hers in a couple of bites and is twisting the wrapper back and forth, desperate to speak, but she knows this is a story I have to tell.

'It started when Chloe couldn't get into live-learning,' I say. 'That was the first weird thing to happen.'

I explain how my parents seemed worried, on edge. About how I'd hacked into the pharma system. About Violet.

He listens, his chin resting on his hand, his eyes on mine. He doesn't react, apart from when I mention the hacking. Then his eyes grow wide, but only for a fraction of a second.

The one thing I don't mention at all, is Charlie Scott. Dad asked me not to. Charlie Scott doesn't seem so important right now, anyway.

'Mum and Dad have—' I hesitate. 'All digital trace of Mum and Dad has been erased. They have no credits and no connection. It's like they never existed. I don't think Chloe can get her medicine,' I add quietly.

I tell him that I'd planned to go home but realized I could only help my family if I was able to go back into the pharma system and fix what I'd done.

'Then the principal called me in. She said that my weekly credits had stopped. She was going to send me home anyway. That's when I asked you if I could come here. My port connection has been deactivated. I could only use the school's and I was about to lose that, too. I thought that here, maybe I could use your school connection, that no one would be searching for me and I would have more time.'

'OK,' says Finn. 'Hiding three people is going to take a bit of planning. But what else can I do?' He frowns. 'I mean, I'm no good at programming, that kind of stuff.'

'I am.'

He turns to Violet. Her face is pale. There are grey shadows beneath her eyes. But her defiant expression has returned.

'Come on, I thought we didn't have much time,' interrupts Mae, unable to stay quiet any longer. 'You said you needed more than three days, Jess, but doesn't Violet have to be back at school by eight a.m? It took us seven hours to walk here, so,' she pauses to look at her port-watch, 'we should have left thirty minutes ago.'

'I'll have to be reported missing first,' says Violet.

'Reassuring,' says Mae, but there is no hard edge to her voice any more.

Finn runs his fingers through his thick brown hair, pushing it away from his forehead. For the first time tonight, he seems uneasy. 'So, what do you need first—a port-com, or somewhere to hide?' he asks.

I open my backpack and pass my port-com to him. 'I brought mine. Can you connect me?' I ask, my heart thumping faster. The familiar heavy feeling has returned. Once I have a connection, I'm not sure where to begin.

Violet reaches for her waterproof suit and unzips the pockets, taking out a black cylinder and a small box.

'I brought mine, too,' she says, pressing something in the side of the box. A screen hologram appears, hovering mid-air in front of her. She unfurls a keyboard and places it on the floor by her feet. 'This has the most sophisticated Virtual Private Network available. I've modified the encryptions so that even my father's cybersecurity agents can't crack it.

'But then I've accessed my father's network so many times, I'm not sure I should call them "security" agents. I can almost do it with my eyes shut.' She glances at me.

Suddenly I realize why Violet is so confident, why she's so sure she can help me. The pharma system she 'hacked' is part of her father's organization. That's why she—JP—managed to solve my challenge so quickly. She knew what to do. She could almost do it *with her eyes shut*. She just waited a few days so that I wouldn't be too suspicious.

A flicker of hope grows in my chest. Hope that we can reinstate my parents. Hope that we won't need three days, maybe not even one.

'I broke into the system a few years ago,' Violet continues.

I almost get the feeling that she's enjoying herself.

'I sent Dad a port-message with an embedded file. A picture of some art project I'd done. My port-address was in his list of "safe" contacts. When he clicked on the file, it infected his port-com with spyware. I was able to copy his passwords and access the system to the highest level without even needing to hack it. He never suspected that his own daughter would use his email address to hack the company system.'

'But—why would you want to hack your own father's company?' says Mae.

'Not everyone in my family believes deletion is the answer to cybercrime. I don't like what his company does. How it treats people. How *he* treats people.'

Violet begins to type. I place my port-com down on a box of paper towels. There's no point in attempting to hack the system. Not when Violet has a password.

After a few minutes, she asks me to join her. Side by side, we work together using the hovering display to access the sector of the database where I saw my parents' names. Where I left a trace.

'Errm.'

Mae's voice makes me jump. I was concentrating on the numbers and symbols hovering in front of me. I'd almost forgotten she was there.

'I don't want to interrupt,' she says, 'but its six a.m. Do we have a plan?'

Finn gets to his feet. 'The cooks will be here soon,' he whispers. 'The kitchen is next door.'

'Will they come in here?' asks Mae.

'I don't know. This isn't a food store, but maybe the cleaners will need something.'

Violet hasn't looked up from what she's doing.

'Can we keep going?' I ask.

Finn nods. 'Perhaps no talking from now, though.' He walks silently to the door and puts his ear against it, listening.

'Jessica,' says Violet, oblivious to what Finn has just said.

'Shhh,' Mae and I hiss together.

Violet ignores us. 'Is this you?' She points at the display.

I sit back down. Hovering in front of me is the same text I saw just over two weeks ago. The list of names, next to a row of tags. I see Dad's name, only this time, instead of the R8 tag, in brackets after his name is the letter <D>.

'He's been flagged,' says Violet, pointing to the 'D'. 'You'd think such a smart group of people would come up with a better flag for 'deleted' than <D>.' She turns to look at me. 'What was there before? Which cipher?

The account is inert. The only way I can reinstate it without triggering an alarm is to revert to what was there previously.'

Finn waves at me from the door and puts his finger to his lips.

I draw R8 on the floor with my finger.

Violet nods. She finally seems to have realized that we need to be quiet.

I rub the dust from my fingertip. When I look up, Violet is in a different area of the system. I look more closely. It's coding for the tags, allowing you to alter them at source—without leaving a trace. The area I had been trying to find. I point to it and mouth 'How?'

She ignores me and carries on. After a few minutes, she returns to the first screen, and points. My father's name is there, followed by R8. The delete flag has gone.

I turn to look at Violet. She smiles. Then she gives me the thumbs up. Two things I never thought I would see her do.

She has fixed my mess. I feel a tingle in my chest, a kind of warmth, which spreads across my shoulders and down through my body, as the tension of the last few weeks seems to ease a little.

I lean over to hug her, but she shrinks away.

'Thank you,' I whisper.

Those two words don't really feel enough. But Violet doesn't seem interested anyway. She is watching something across the room.

Out of the corner of my eye, I notice Finn waving at us. He is backing slowly from the door. I hear footsteps, and the sound of something being placed on the floor. Silently, Mae and I follow Finn behind a rack of shelving. Violet presses the side of her port-com and the hologram vanishes. She hurries to join us, but the tube slips from her fingers and tinkles to the floor. She moves to fetch it, but Finn pulls her back. The handle on the door moves down, and a man in blue overalls enters the room. He picks up the tube and looks at it curiously, before placing it on the shelf, then he pauses. He picks up Mae's waterproof, then turns round, looking for the owner of the wet clothing.

Violet's knee presses into my shoulder. I hardly dare to breathe. For a few seconds, the room is utterly silent. I think the man is going to come over, but instead he gathers up the other wet things and leaves the room. He doesn't notice my port-com, or the backpack lying on the floor nearby.

'We have to get out of here,' says Finn. 'He's going to come back. If he thinks students have been using the room, he might decide to lock it.'

'Violet's finished,' I whisper. 'She's reinstated my parents.'

'In four hours?' whispers Finn. 'Instead of three days?'

Mae jumps in the air and does a silent fist pump, then grabs Violet and hugs her before she has time to move away.

'Seriously, though,' says Finn, 'we have to get out of here.'

Almost immediately, my elation ebbs. Violet has reinstated my parents, but how will they realize? And what has happened to them in the last sixteen days? The urge to go home is stronger than ever. But at this very moment there is probably a search party out looking for Violet.

'Maybe one of us can sneak past the kitchens, but not four of us,' says Finn. 'Everyone will know you're not pupils here.'

'Well,' says Violet, 'maybe I should just wait for the cleaner to come back. I don't mind if he finds me. My father will send someone to look for me anyway.'

'But then they'll find all of us!' says Mae. 'How do we explain running away from school, and ending up here? We'll be in so much trouble. They might decide we're a bad influence on the other kids; send us home to use live-learning for ever. And what about Finn? He'll get into trouble too!'

My chest feels tight. This isn't Violet's fault. It's mine. Violet's fixed things for me, but I've messed up everything for Mae and Finn. I can't do any more live-learning. I can't leave school. An image of the music room flashes through my head. What about the competition? What about Jack?

'I should go home,' I hear myself say.

'But I thought you *shouldn't* go home?' says Mae exasperated. 'Fine,' she adds, 'then I'll come with you. That would be better than waiting here for Violet's father.'

'The principal sent Jess home,' says Violet. 'That's where school expects her to be. If you go too, then how do you explain it? It will draw attention to the real reason we all left.'

'Marvellous. So you're suggesting it would be better all-round if I wait here with you? While your dad tracks us down, then speaks nicely to the principal about how I corrupted you?'

'If you want,' says Violet. 'That can be arranged. I had something different in mind. I was planning to say that I'd persuaded you to help me run away. There was someone on ROOM who I wanted to meet for real. Someone who went to this school. That you hadn't wanted to do it, but I'd talked you into it.'

Mae's mouth is hanging open. Finn looks from Mae to Violet, frowning slightly.

'You mean—' Mae hesitates. 'You mean you're going to say that this is all your fault?'

'Basically,' says Violet. 'It feels like the logical thing to do. You do have a ROOM account, don't you?' she adds, looking at Finn.

He hesitates, trying, like me, to take everything in. 'Yes, but I never use it.'

'Well, we probably need to add some stuff to it then, to make it look "lived in". We'd better make sure you're one of my ROOMmates, too.'

Finn unclips his port-watch and passes it to Violet. 'Based on the last few hours, I think you'll be faster at fixing my ROOM than I will.'

I feel as if I'm listening and watching the others through a veil, between the real and the cyber, the hidden and the shared. I can't work out which side I'm on. All the different parts of me seem to have collided in this storeroom. My body aches with exhaustion, my mind does too. I need to go home. I need to see Chloe.

'Jess, I could try and find somewhere for you to hide out—at least until tomorrow. You could rest first,' says Finn. He runs his fingers through his hair, like always, when he's not sure what to do.

In that split-second I see that Finn is glad I am here. That he misses me, like I miss him. I take a deep breath. 'I need to go today.' I pick up my backpack and port-com. 'It's half the distance I walked last night. It will be easier in daylight, too.'

'OK. Then you have to leave right now. You know the way back to the bathroom window?' He scrambles to his feet and heads to the door. Pressing one ear against the wood to listen for sounds in the corridor outside.

'What about you? Won't you get into trouble for letting Mae and Violet into school?'

'He has to go back to his dormitory. Obviously.' Violet interrupts. 'Mae and I broke into the school by ourselves. Finn had no idea we were coming.'

'Obviously.' I smile at Violet.

End 2

The ground is muddy from last night's rain. A carpet of yellow-orange bracken stops me slipping as I pick my way alongside the farmer's fence. It feels strange to be alone. For the first half an hour, I turn round to check that Violet and Mae are keeping up.

After a while, I am walking with a steady rhythm, stopping only to sip some water. I sense that I'm close to home. The hills are familiar. I recognize a spinney of trees. From the next hill, I should be able to see the gully, our treehouse hidden within, the meadow rising up beyond.

My footsteps quicken until I break into a jog, my port-com thumping gently on my back. I feel my legs burning, and the blisters on my feet sting, even though Finn gave me his dry socks. I don't care, though. All I can think about is seeing Chloe. Hugging Mum and Dad.

I run down the hill, holding my arms out like Finn did, the morning we left for school. I keep running, past the treehouse, and up through the meadow. My breath is coming in ragged gasps. I feel as if my legs are about to give way. Past the beehives, through the gate. Everything looks so normal, so peaceful. It doesn't reflect the last two weeks, how I've felt, or what has happened. The house comes into view. I pause and rest my hands on my knees, trying to catch my breath.

After a minute or so, I start moving again, walking slowly. Several of the vegetable patches have been freshly dug. A coil of rope and some willow stakes lie on the path. Outside the back door is a stack of glass jars. Way more than we usually need.

I push open the door, and step inside. The house feels cold. There is no warm bread smell. No one in the kitchen. Perhaps I passed them, working in the fields. I try to calm down, to stop moving for a moment and think. On the table is a chopping board and several bowls containing greenish pastes. There is a familiar scent, too. Not food, or baking–eucalyptus.

I hear something moving upstairs. Someone. All logical thought flies from my head and I run towards the stairs, taking them two at a time. On the landing I look left then right, trying to locate the sound. The door to my bedroom creaks open and Mum steps out. There are shadows beneath her eyes. She rests her hand on the door handle, as if supporting herself. She looks exhausted.

'Jess!' she says softly. 'Are you OK?' She holds out her arms, and I rush towards her.

'Are you in trouble?' she asks, her voice wavering.

I shake my head gently, as it rests on her shoulder. She doesn't need to know everything right now. After a few seconds, she lets me go, leaning once more on the door handle.

'I'm sorry we haven't been able to contact you. It's been so awful–it's–.' She stops talking and puts her hand to her forehead.

I peer past her, to my room.

'Chloe's in there,' she says. 'We've tried everything we can think of, but she's not doing well. We don't have any medicine left.' A tightness grips my chest. 'And we've nearly run out of home-made remedies. They're not really working, anyway.' She smiles weakly. 'You can go in. Try not to wake her.' Mum moves aside.

I step past her, into my room.

There is a strong smell of eucalyptus, mixed with frankincense. Dad is sitting on the floor next to the bunk bed, a cup in his hand. Beside him, propped up on several cushions, is Chloe. Her eyes are closed, and her skin white. Her lips are pale, blueish. Her breathing is shallow.

I feel the colour drain from my own face. This is my fault. If I hadn't been so careless, Chloe wouldn't be this poorly. I stare at her for a few minutes before Dad gets up.

He puts his hand on my shoulder, and whispers, 'Let's go downstairs for a minute. I need a drink of water.'

Mum is already in the kitchen, over by the sink, filling glasses with water.

Dad pulls up a chair by the old wooden table. He seems exhausted, like Mum. He looks at me and takes a deep breath, in and out.

'Jessica, I know you have some things to tell us. How you got here. What's going on at school. But as long as you are OK, that can wait,' he says. 'We need to talk to you. Urgently. Chloe is very unwell. You know that she can go through a rough patch, which, unless we treat it early, is more likely to spiral into something serious. We were managing her symptoms, but then,' he pauses to take a sip of water from the glass which Mum has passed him, 'then we ran out of medicine.'

'And we can't order any more,' adds Mum quietly. 'Our accounts seem to have closed down. Nothing works. We were almost out of credits, but we had enough for one more delivery. Then everything shut down.'

'There's no power,' Dad says. His eyes are bright with a strange, fierce sort of energy.

I can't bear to listen any longer. To sit here any more, doing nothing. I slide the backpack from my shoulders, and take out my port-com.

'It has power,' I say, as they stare at it, confused. I can't tell them more. Not yet. Not until I know whether it's worked.

Mum and Dad exchange a look.

'Jess, it's not just the power,' Mum adds, quietly. 'It's everything.'

I push aside some of the bowls and place my port-com on the kitchen table in front of Dad. My mouth feels dry. What if something went wrong when Violet fixed what I'd done? What if it didn't work, or she left a new trace, and they've just deleted Dad again?

'Try to access your credit portal,' I say, turning the screen so that it's facing him.

He puts his head in his hands. 'Darling, it won't work. Nothing works.'

'Just try it. Please.'

Dad breathes out slowly, rubbing his forehead with his fingertips.

He begins to type. After a few seconds he sits up in his chair, glancing up at Mum again.

He leans back, blinking at the screen in front of him. Then he turns to look at me. The fierceness in his eyes has been replaced by something else. He looks bewildered.

'Jess,' he shakes his head, 'how did you do this?'

'What?' asks Mum, sounding alarmed.

Dad is still looking at me. The faintest smile lifting the corners of his mouth.

'It *was* you, wasn't it?'

'It was more of a team effort,' I say.

'Please tell me what's happened,' says Mum.

'Walk towards the lamp,' Dad replies.

Mum gets to her feet and takes a few steps towards the lamp. The sensor clicks and it begins to glow. She gasps, lifting a hand to her mouth.

'Try the port-screen,' I say.

With new energy, Mum rushes to the learning room, Dad and I following close behind.

She taps the screen and whispers, 'Live-learning,' as if this might be some kind of joke.

A timetable appears.

She gasps again. 'Does—everything work?' Her voice is shaking, like earlier.

'Our credit account has reappeared,' says Dad. 'I've

reactivated our payments. Everything should work. Jess, how did you know what to do?' he asks quietly.

Suddenly, I feel so weak that I'm not sure my legs can hold me up. I haven't eaten since the energy bar early this morning. I haven't slept since the day before.

'Look at her, she's exhausted,' says Mum, 'and hungry, I bet.'

'Food can wait,' I say. 'You'll be able to order Chloe's medicine now. Make sure you use Rapid Drone Service.'

Shock 2

As Dad prepares something to eat, the kitchen comes slowly back to life, filling with warmth from the stove and the smell of cooking. Dad asks me what happened, why I'm not at school, but I'm desperate to hear what's been happening at home, first.

Mum goes upstairs every few minutes to check on Chloe.

Meanwhile, Dad explains they planned to take honey to a supplier who promised a good price in exchange for flour and some other things, but the transport was dead. After that, nothing worked at all. They used beeswax candles at night and rationed the fuel for cooking. Outside, they planted more winter crops—enough to be completely self-sufficient, but they would take time to grow. Indoors, they were mostly wrapped in blankets, working in shifts to watch Chloe. This morning, Chloe took a turn for the worse.

After an hour or so, I hear the familiar sound of a drone. Dad rushes from the kitchen to collect the delivery.

Chloe's medicine.

I feel my eyes begin to close as waves of tiredness flow through my body. I want to stay here and wait for Dad to return. But sleep seems to be taking over. I decide to curl up on the bench outside for a bit. The air is cold, but wintery sunshine dapples the herb beds. I wrap myself in several blankets. It's peaceful out here. Calm.

I feel someone gently rocking my shoulder. The sun has set, and the sky is fading from dark blue to night. I shiver a little.

'Come on, sleepy head,' says Dad's voice, gently. 'Follow me.'

'OK,' I answer, wearily.

I stretch out my legs. My right foot is numb from where it's been pressing on the arm of the bench. I realize that the day is almost over, and tomorrow is Monday. By Thursday, Jack and I were supposed to send in our final recording.

I stamp my feet to get my circulation moving. A soft light glows through the kitchen window. I head towards it like a large, blanket-patterned moth.

As I walk upstairs, I wonder whether Mae and Violet are back at school, if they're having dinner, or sitting in the principal's office, explaining exactly where they've been, and why. Instinctively I glance down at my port-watch. It's no longer blank but has the pale glow which shows it's merely sleeping. In the corner I can see that I have a message from Violet.

Check your encrypted msgs. Have sent link to that 'area' you were interested in.

I'll have to check it later.

I follow Dad into the bedroom. Chloe is propped against the pillows, her face pale, her eyes open. I rush over and wrap my arms around her, listening to the gentle rattle in her chest.

'Don't say anything,' I whisper. 'You need to save your breath right now. You can annoy me with lots of questions when you're better.'

I perch on the edge of the bed, and tell Chloe about Gala Night, and the hologram tiger cubs. Things I know she would love to hear about. After half an hour or so, her eyes begin to close again.

'Night night,' I whisper.

Chloe nods.

'Goodnight, Kit Cat,' I say bending down to stroke Kit, who is curled around her feet.

I pull the door closed behind me, then pause, my

fingertips resting on the handle. Violet may have fixed my mess, but I haven't stopped Chloe's medicine from getting more expensive all the time—the reason I hacked Global Connections in the first place. When this delivery runs out, I wonder whether my parents can afford any more.

I head downstairs, then drift from room to room, while I wait for Mum or Dad to reappear. In the snug are two glass lanterns. There is a faint smell of honey from the beeswax candles within. Piles of blankets lie on the sofa and the chairs. Jam jars containing smaller candles with blackened wicks are dotted along the edges of the hall floor. I don't know what I was expecting to see when I came home. If you delete someone virtually, I guess there's no scene of devastation. It takes a little time for the real person to fade. Unless one of you is ill.

I push open the door to Mum and Dad's office, breathing in its papery, leathery smell. There are several gaps on the shelves, left by the books which Dad gave me.

'I don't know what we'd have done, Jess, if you hadn't come home today.'

I didn't hear Dad coming. He joins me in the doorway, staring at the family treasure.

'Chloe couldn't have soldiered on for much longer without proper treatment. Perhaps now, we can stabilize her condition. She can begin her recovery. But–' He pauses, as if he can't find the right words. 'We may still not have enough,' he says. 'I thought you should know.'

I think of Jack. How he had a supply at school for the entire term. How can it be so different for us?

'And Jess, Mum and I still need to talk to you.' Dad smiles at me, but the smile doesn't reach his eyes.

I feel my face flush. Perhaps they know. Perhaps they've guessed that I was the reason they were plunged into darkness, with no power, no credits, no way of proving that they existed at all.

'Let's go to the snug,' he says. 'Mum's waiting there.'

Dad joins Mum on the sofa. I sit in the armchair, my heart thumping. Part of me knew I couldn't keep my hacking secret from them for ever. I just wish they didn't have to find out this way.

'Jess,' says Dad, 'there are some things you need to know.'

I take a deep breath, trying to slow the pounding in my chest.

'Some things about me.'

I look from Dad to Mum. This isn't how I expected the conversation to start.

'I should probably go back to the beginning.'

Dad hesitates, as if making a decision, then gently clears his throat.

'I never worked as a farmer. That wasn't my job. I used to be a programmer.'

I hear myself gasp, feel my mouth hang open as I stare at Dad, watching for some sign that he's making this up, that he's joking. Dad carries on talking, as if he hasn't noticed.

'I worked for the biggest tech company, making a lot of money for them and for me.' He pauses. 'When antibiotics began to fail, and resistant bacteria spread, at first it was a disaster. Chaos. No one wanted to risk hurting themselves and getting an infection or picking up a resistant strain. Then, it became an opportunity.

'Keep people at home, and they spend all their money via the portals—port-com, port-watch, port-screen. If you control the portals, that money is yours. The bigger companies swallowed up the smaller ones, until almost everything was controlled by Global Connections. They had big plans. Complex algorithms to ensure they received the highest possible percentage of people's incomes. To make sure everyone's earnings were funnelled towards them.' Dad is speaking quickly, as if the words are fighting to get out.

'They harvested people's data down to the smallest details, like your favourite colour, or whether you were scared of the dark, then they used it to sell you things. The goal was to turn your home into a kind of shopfront. Your every whim converted into a product to purchase.

'I was leading the team developing those algorithms. Then someone came up with a new idea. A new algorithm. One which made sure the tech companies took *everything* you earned. If you didn't spend much on food, then they would charge you more for clothes, if you didn't spend much on clothes, then they would charge you more for healthcare plans. No one knew what anyone else was paying, and so no one was suspicious. The algorithm meant that it was done subtly, too, so you barely noticed the change. I should have left earlier, but this was the last straw. I didn't want to be part of a plan to basically steal people's money. I handed in my resignation, but they wouldn't let me leave. They said I knew too much.' Dad pauses and looks at Mum.

She gently nods her head, as if encouraging Dad to carry on.

'So I had to disappear. The tech organization hired people to find me. I changed my name. I moved house. I had to reinvent myself.' He hesitates. 'Charlie Scott was me. The *old* me.'

I gasp. 'So that's why your name was in the trunk?'

'Jess, I thought they'd finally tracked me down. That we had been deleted because someone had discovered my real identity. I could still do the organization a lot of damage. So, what I don't understand, is how *you* managed to fix it?'

I take another deep breath. 'Dad, there are a few things you need to know about me, too.'

Data

I show Dad the little grey book. I explain how I taught myself to programme, then taught myself to hack.

Mum and Dad listen, their faces showing no signs of surprise.

'I hacked into the administration system for Chloe's medicine. I made a stupid mistake. But my port-com is protected. It's almost impossible to locate. The problem was, I altered your records. My mistake led directly back to you—and any account associated with you. That's how I knew what had happened. I made it happen. I'm sorry.'

'But why were you looking at that system in the first place, Jess?' asks Dad.

'I knew that the price of the medicine kept going up. I wanted to see if I could do something to help.

To change what we pay. To change something. Dad, what was the name of the algorithm they developed?'

For the first time, he looks surprised. 'It was called the Data Treaty.'

All the air seems to have been sucked from the room.

'The Data Treaty?' My mind is whirring. 'The Data Treaty is why Chloe's medicine goes up all the time? The Data Treaty has realized that's the only thing we spend money on. So whenever we have spare credits, the price goes up?'

I realize now, that we can never win. Never have enough.

Mum and Dad are silent.

I need to stand up, to pace around the room—to do something other than just sit here. Then I remember the message from Violet.

Have sent link to that 'area' you were interested in.

I should ignore it. When I tried to fix things before, it almost cost me everything I care about. But Dad said they can't afford the right treatment for Chloe. And thanks to the Data Treaty, that will never change. I make up my mind.

'What if I could fool the algorithm into thinking that we spend more on other things? What if I could fool it—so that we pay less for Chloe's medicine?'

Still, no one says anything.

'Would you let me do it?'

Mum speaks first. 'Jess, you are playing with fire. Global Connections swallows up everything. It will swallow us up too, given the slightest chance. I think you know that now.'

'That's true,' says Dad. 'I tried to hide from them, to live without them as much as I could. But we're still victims of their greed. Of their algorithms.'

I nod, but I don't say anything. I don't want to upset Mum or Dad, but my mind is made up. I know what I have to do.

Beginning 2

I return to school on Tuesday afternoon.

No one says much, but that's not unusual. I catch the other girls in the dormitory looking at me, though, when they think I won't notice. Around school, I see people scanning me on their port-phones too. I guess there are rumours. I don't know where from, or what they are, but Violet hasn't come back yet, and no one has said where she is, so people make up stuff.

I realize that I miss her.

Mae seems to be generating a lot of interest, too, which she takes in her stride. She has even begun asking for credits when she catches people scanning her.

Although it was hard to leave home again, it wasn't as hard as I thought. Also, I didn't have any choice. The 'credit issue' had been resolved, and so the principal expected me back. Maybe when the worst things you can imagine have happened already, it's difficult to feel anxious about very much. I know I'm going to see Chloe again soon, for half term. Finn will be there too. And Mae. Chloe is beside herself with excitement. We've promised Mae's family that we won't keep her for the whole of the holiday. Just until she's earned her keep in the garden.

I've seen Jack, too. We recorded our piece for the music competition. It wasn't perfect, but Miss Singer was happy. We have decided to carry on with the extra tuition, both me and Jack. I spend most evenings playing or composing. I don't have much time for hacking. I miss Violet, but strangely I don't really miss JP.

Although I did go back into the pharma system. Once. I used Violet's password and followed her link to change the tag on Dad's name—properly. It's now the same as Tom Merril's. I don't fully understand the Data Treaty algorithm, yet, but it's clear that Jack's family didn't only buy medicine, flour and shoes. The algorithm seems happy we are spending most of our credits on other things. The price of Chloe's medicine has halved in a week, and we've begun to receive random free samples too. Floor cleaner, socks, toothpaste. I haven't fixed the system, but at least I've found a loophole.

Mum said taking on big corporations is playing with fire. She says you can't speak truth to power. Dad tried. But hiding from them, pretending they don't exist, doesn't seem to work either.

I need to think logically, like Violet. Perhaps there is a third way.

Mae's mum quietly started her school, and people came.

Violet refused to follow in her father's footsteps.

I saved Chloe—in the end. Maybe I can do the same for other families like ours.

I guess change doesn't have to start big. Because small things grow. But it can only begin, if you want to make it happen.

MORE FROM ELE FOUNTAIN